LION HUNT

RUTH KIRTLEY

Scripture Union

Other books by the same author:
Brainbox

Copyright © Ruth Kirtley 2000
First published 2000

Scripture Union, 207–209 Queensway, Bletchley,
Milton Keynes, MK2 2EB, England.

ISBN 1 85999 412 1

All rights reserved. No part of this publication
may be reproduced, stored in a retrieval system,
or transmitted in any form or by any means,
electronic, mechanical, photocopying, recording
or otherwise, without the prior permission of
Scripture Union.

The right of Ruth Kirtley to be identified as
author of this work has been asserted by her in
accordance with the Copyright, Designs and
Patents Act 1988.

British Library Cataloguing-in-Publication Data.
A catalogue record of this book is available from
the British Library.

Printed and bound in Great Britain by Creative
Print and Design (Wales) Ebbw Vale.

For St Andrew's Trailblazers
who have given me ideas.

Chapter 1

Tick-eek-tock, tick-eek-tock... The old car's windscreen wipers struggled against the heavy rain. Ashley felt as though he and Patrick were travelling through a never-ending car wash.

He stared through the window beside him, but there was nothing new to look at, just cars, soggy fields and endless rain. He sighed.

"Not much further now," said Patrick sympathetically. "We go off at the next junction."

"Funny," he continued. "I can't understand where this rain has come from. The forecast was fine for today ... It's OK at Edgbaston," he added, nodding towards the radio which burbled quietly. "Australia have been batting all afternoon."

"Mm," Ashley felt a bit shy and wasn't sure what to say. Patrick seemed to understand and tried to keep talking.

"Hungry?"

"A bit."

"Any toffees left?"

Lunch had been at a service area, miles ago, *years* ago. The sun had been shining then. They'd sat at a table smeared with ketchup from someone else's burger. It had been noisy and hot, and Ashley had been glad to get back into the car.

He rummaged along the shelf in front of him,

among the junk that collects in cars on long journeys, and found a bag.

"Here's one," he said, passing a toffee across.

"Good man," Patrick murmured, unwrapping it awkwardly.

Just as well we're in the slow lane, thought Ashley as the car drifted sideways and juddered over the cat's eyes between the lanes. He straightened his baseball cap, flicked a crumb off the knee of his jeans and looked down at his new trainers.

They look good. Wonder if any of the Spookz have got these yet? Did I pack the battery-charger for my Game Boy?

He thought back to earlier that day when Patrick – tall and stooped, with fair wispy hair – had arrived to collect him from home.

There had been a bit of a rush in the morning, Ashley remembered as he unwrapped a toffee. Mum was still ironing clothes to be packed and the twins were getting underfoot. Going away had seemed quite exciting then, but now he just felt tired and fed up.

What's it going to be like? Why did I say I'd come? I could have looked after myself OK at home ... I could even have gone to Gran's with the twins. This could be a Big Mistake!

A few weeks before the end of the summer term Mum had heard from Dad. He was working in Saudi Arabia for six months. He had been doing this sort of thing for as long as Ashley could remember – three months on this job, five weeks on that job. Ashley knew that the money was good, but Dad's work always came first and everything else had to fit in around it. Dad would go away and they settled into their Dad-less routine, then back he'd come and everyone had to readjust until he went away again. Ashley was used to this, but it made Mum grumpy because it was hard to plan things like holidays or study time for her university course.

He watched Mum's face grow tense as she talked on the phone.

"Oh, *wonderful!*" she muttered grimly when the call was over. "There's been a hold-up. Dad probably won't be home till the middle of August."

"What about France?" said Ashley.

"Oh, he'll be back by then," Mum sighed. "Just as well we booked for the end of the month. But what am I going to do with the three of you till then? I've got two essays to write before next term, and Dad was going to look after you all for a bit and give me some peace to work." She sounded a bit worked-up now.

"We can look after ourselves," suggested Ashley.

"No, that wouldn't work," said Mum. "Who'd feed you and mind the twins? We'll need to make survival plans!"

So they did. Gran was delighted to see her grandchildren and said they were welcome to stay as long as they liked, but she was a practical woman.

"Won't Ashley find it rather boring, dear?" she said on the phone later that day.

"I could look after myself here," he suggested to Mum.

"You most certainly could *not!*" Mum replied. "You're only eleven. Goodness knows what you'd get up to! Gran's right, though. You need to be with someone your own age. Let me think!"

Later, she came to Ashley, looking pleased.

"How would you like to stay with the Butterworths?"

"Who?"

"You know, Patrick and Tessa. They popped in at Christmas, on their way home from visiting family."

"Oh, you mean the Boffin!" said Ashley. Mum laughed.

"Well, I suppose Patrick does look a bit like an absent-minded professor, but he and Tessa are great fun. We were all students together and they're some of our oldest friends."

"*Ancient!*" said Ashley.

"Very funny," said Mum, but this time she wasn't laughing. "Anyway, what do you think? They're living in the country now, running a sort of guest house apparently. They've often invited us down to see them, so I rang Tessa and she says they'd be really pleased to have you. It'll be company for their Rachel, too. You used to play so nicely together when you were little."

Ashley winced. Mum could be so embarrassing sometimes. He remembered liking Rachel, though. She wasn't like most of the girls at school. They talked about boys and were always doing each other's hair, but she was interested in football.

"I s'pose so," he said cautiously. "How long?"

"A week or so. The quieter it is here, the quicker I'll be finished," said Mum eagerly.

"But what would we *do*? If it's the country it'll be miles from anywhere, and that means there'll be no shops or cinema or anything."

Mum swept his doubts aside quickly. "Oh, you'll love it, I'm sure!" she said enthusiastically. "They have a river running through the garden and woods to explore. There'll be lots of clean, healthy air; much better for you than this dirty city. And Tessa is a wonderful cook. Go on, what do you say?"

She's making it sound like a "Famous Five" story! A river? Woods? Big deal!

"Why can't I just go to Gran's with the twins?" he tried once more.

"Oh, Ashley, please!" Mum begged. "I want you to have something special, just for you – a chance to get away from having to do four-year-old things with Sam and Joe." Ashley hadn't thought of that. Suddenly the idea didn't seem quite so bad.

There was also another big reason why Ashley had thought this holiday might be a good idea.

It'll give me a chance to get away from Jax and the Spookz for a bit. I need time to think; to decide.

Steve Jackson and his gang were well-known at school; they were really Hard Men. They wore cool clothes and cheeked teachers and didn't do their homework. They weren't into armed hold-ups or stealing cars yet, but they were always boasting about the things they'd nicked from local shops; and everyone knew that they'd sprayed the graffiti on the wall by the main school gate.

They aren't exactly popular with the other kids because they sometimes push people around, but they get respect, and selling stuff they've got from the shops means they've always got more money than anyone else. That'd be great.

Ashley wasn't sure if he really wanted to be in the Spookz, but Jax had come up to him in the lunch queue one day and given him this look. "I've been watching you, man. You could be one of us ... Know what I'm sayin'?"

Maybe it was his size that had made Jax notice him. Being tall for his age and quite heavily-built, Ashley looked tougher than he was. You only got into the Spookz by invitation and it was quite something to be noticed by them. It was exciting but it needed thinking about, because you had to pass the Test first; show you were serious and had guts. Jax decided what you had to do. Ashley knew for a fact that Ollie Patterson was caught in the school canteen with four pieces of pizza up his jacket that he hadn't paid for, even though he had plenty of money in his pocket. Then he'd seen Alex Benson shouting at Hulk, the toughest boy in year nine. He'd come to school next day with a massive black eye, but he was one of the Spookz now.

Will I pass the Test? Do I really want to? Will it be worth it?

Ashley couldn't decide what to do. He was happy enough. At school he did OK and he had good mates, John and Richie. But if he joined the Spookz he'd be someone special – have excitement, get respect. Trouble was, he'd also be a marked man at school. Whenever there was trouble, the Spookz always got blamed and some kids were scared of them ... *really* scared.

Sometimes I think it'd be great, but I want to stay friends with John and Richie. I don't want little kids being scared of me and I don't really want trouble! But what happens if I say no to Jax? He knows where I live and he's waiting for an answer.

The fact was, Ashley was a bit scared of the

Spookz himself. Yes, he definitely needed time to think and Mum was still waiting.

"OK then," he sighed. So it was arranged.

Patrick had been on a quick visit to his parents nearby and collected Ashley on his way home. Now here they were, far from Ashley's house on the smart new estate just beyond the tall buildings and busy streets of the city, leaving the motorway and heading into the heart of the countryside.

"Ah," sighed Patrick, "I always feel better when I leave the traffic behind."

Soon they were chugging along narrow, twisting roads.

"Oh dear," muttered Patrick as he peered at the rain. "This isn't a very good start to your holiday."

Ashley thought about the comics and tapes and his Game Boy that went everywhere with him. He'd packed them himself in the back-pack at his feet. He'd come well prepared, but if it kept raining like this he'd be running out of things to do in a couple of days.

"Is there a town near where you live? You know, shops 'n' that?"

"Depends what you call near, I suppose. Our nearest town is about six miles away. We go there for the supermarket and things like the dentist. Rachel's school is there, too. But there's a small shop in the village and that's quite near – only about one and a half miles down the road."

"One and a half *miles*?" gasped Ashley in disbelief. "That's *near*?"

Patrick chuckled.

"It takes no time at all on a bike. Rachel goes there often. You can borrow a bike and go with her."

On and on they drove. The world seemed very empty.

Where are we going? Where is everybody? I feel like I'm going to tip over the edge of the world in a minute!

"Nearly there now," said Patrick.

They turned off the main road and into an even narrower one – a farm track really. Bumping downhill, wet ferns and grass slapped against the side of the car. Ashley thought about the new four-wheel-drive people-carrier Dad had bought a few months ago.

He'd eat this track for breakfast! This old thing's going to fall apart in a minute!

"This is our short cut," Patrick was explaining. "There's another way in off the main road, but I thought you'd enjoy this. Hold tight!"

The car dived down and across a shallow, swiftly-running river, water splashing up on either side. Ashley forgot to be critical and grinned with delight.

"Great!"

"You arrived on the right day," said Patrick. "Two days ago the ford was only a trickle, but all this rain has made a big difference. Here we are, this is Yaffle House."

The car had been climbing a steepish hill and now turned in through a gateway of tall stone pillars. Through the blurred windscreen loomed a big ivy-covered house with many windows.

"Home at last!" sighed Patrick with relief as he stopped the car at a solid-looking front door with a shiny brass knocker. Ashley suddenly felt uncomfortable. Patrick seemed to understand and smiled gently.

12

"We're really glad to have you, Ashley," he said. "I expect it'll feel a bit quiet at first, but things don't stay quiet for long with Rachel about ... and here she is!"

A small figure came leaping down the front steps, with a little black dog at her heels. She wrenched the car door open and dragged Patrick from his seat. The three figures merged in a noisy, laughing hug.

"Dad! You're home just in time! Mum said if you weren't here in the next half hour she was going to give your tea to the chickens!" A fresh squall of rain spattered down as Ashley climbed stiffly from his seat, nervously pulling down the peak of his cap. Another figure had joined them, and there was laughter and more hugs.

"You're here at last!"

"This weather's *unbelievable!*"

"Hello, Ashley! Quick, into the house before you're soaked!"

Chapter 2

"Rachel, close the door, for goodness sake!"

"What *rain!*"

"How was your journey?"

"Grab the Mole before he dances dirty paw-marks over the floor!"

Standing in the hall, Ashley felt surrounded by people, and it took him a few moments to get the blur of voices and faces into focus. Then he recognised Tessa. She was small with short dark hair and eyes that crinkled up when she laughed.

"Hello, Ashley, I hardly recognised you. Your mum said you'd grown, but goodness...!" She hugged him. "It's lovely to see you. How are those little brothers of yours? Rachel, *please* hold on to Moley – he's getting over-excited!"

Rachel, also small and dark with cropped hair, grinned in welcome as she struggled with the wriggling, wet dog.

"Hi, Ash!"

Ashley smiled back and shifted awkwardly from one foot to the other. He felt exposed, standing there with everyone looking at him. There was no Mum or Dad to answer for him, and no Sam and Joe to distract everyone's attention by looking cute or making a fuss about something. Tessa took charge of the situation.

"Pat, you unpack the car. Rachel, shut the Mole in the living room and then take Ashley up and show him his room. I'll go and put the kettle on and rescue the meal. We'll eat in ten minutes!"

Rachel darted away, opened a door, shut the little dog into the room beyond, then led the way, running up a wide curving staircase. Ashley followed her slowly, carrying his back-pack and half listening as she chattered. He was trying to take in his surroundings.

"Big house," he commented.

"Yes, I s'pose it is," Rachel agreed, "but we don't live in this bit. Most of the rooms in this part are for the guests. We live up at the top of the house and in the bit out the back – the Annexe. We've got our own stairs at the back, but I wanted to bring you up the posh front stairs the first time." She turned to him abruptly and said, "By the way, please don't call me Rachel. It's too ... you know ... I like Ray better, OK?"

"OK, Ray," said Ashley with a smile. She relaxed and grinned back.

"Look at these bannisters!" She stroked the smooth curve of gleaming wood. "Wouldn't they be brilliant to slide down? Mum won't let me. She thinks it'd be dangerous. Still, one day, maybe ... These are all guest bedrooms," she continued, waving a hand around the landing. Ashley looked at all the doors.

"Red Room, Green Room," he read the neat labels on each one.

"Oh, we give each room a colour," Rachel explained. "Dad says it's more friendly than numbers. The guests like it and some of them ask for

15

the same colour each time they come. This way!"

She hurried on along the landing, ran up two steps, turned a corner and vanished through a door marked Private. Beyond was another passage.

"This is the back of the house, part of the Annexe. That's the bathroom, airing cupboard, Mum and Dad's room, and yours is up ... here!" Ashley followed her up another flight of narrow, winding stairs. Through a little window half-way up, he saw grass and flowerbeds far below.

"We must be at the top of the house!" he panted as he caught up with her on a tiny landing.

"Almost!"

"You must have loads of money if you've got such a big house," Ashley said.

"No, I don't think so," Rachel replied. "If we did, we wouldn't have to worry about Pig Face."

"Who's he?"

"Oh, just somebody," Rachel changed the subject. "These are the attics where the servants used to sleep. I think they're the best rooms in the house. That's mine and this is yours!" She pushed open a door and he followed her into a small, white-painted room with a sloping ceiling and a low window that looked out at waving treetops. It was very neat, very plain. There was a bed and a small chest of drawers. A patchwork bedspread made a bright splash of colour, but Ashley's heart sank as he stared around. No football posters, no TV, no computer.

Wish I'd brought more of my stuff with me.

"D'you like it?" Rachel's bright eyes smiled anxiously.

"Oh, yeah. Yeah, it's great," he said hastily. "It's just a bit, well, tidy, I suppose."

"It doesn't *need* to be!" Rachel chuckled. "Come and see this!" She led him out on to the landing and flung open the other door. Ashley gazed in on a glorious jumble of colour. Rachel's room was crammed with posters, models, books and clothes. There were cactus plants on the window-sill, mobiles hanging from the ceiling and barely a space to walk across the floor to her bed. Ashley stared in amazement.

"Doesn't your mum mind?"

"No." Rachel grinned. "She says it's my territory and I can do what I like with it, but I mustn't let any of the mess get past this door!"

Ashley thought about the rows he had with his mum about tidying up. She was always going on about it.

"If they had Tidying Up in the Olympics, my mum'd win the gold medal!" He turned and then stopped. "Who's that?" he asked, pointing at a large black-and-white photograph in a heavy, dark frame which hung on the wall beside Rachel's bed.

"Oh, that's my Great Uncle Leo. He died a few years ago. This was his house. He gave it to us because Dad was his nephew."

Ashley looked at the elderly gentleman in the photo who stared sternly back at him. He had white hair, a neatly clipped moustache and a pointed beard. Beneath the beetling eyebrows a pair of dark eyes seemed to stare right into him. There was something very powerful about their expression.

"Looks like he was strict," he commented.

Rachel screwed up her face and shook her head.

"Weeell, I suppose he was a bit. But he was really good fun, too. We used to come here for our holidays right from when I was a baby. He was great; he liked playing tricks on people. I loved him."

Ashley looked doubtfully at the photo.

There was a loud buzzing sound from outside on the landing. Rachel jumped.

"Oops, that means 'hurry up'!" she said. "There's a buzzer up on the wall, see? It saves people coming upstairs to find me."

They thundered down the back stairs and arrived, panting, in the large living room with tall windows that looked out over the back garden. The rain still fell, but only as drizzle, and somehow the weather seemed more remote now that they were indoors. The table was set and the smell of food made Ashley realise just how hungry he was.

Everyone sat round the table and there was a moment's quiet while Patrick said a prayer. Ashley's hands were already reaching for his knife and fork, and he blushed with embarrassment, but no one noticed.

As they ate, Tessa asked questions about Ashley's family and explained about Yaffle House. Rachel interrupted, but Patrick ate silently, deep in his own thoughts.

"This isn't really an ordinary guest house," Tessa explained. "I suppose you could call it a retreat centre." Ashley looked blank and she smiled as she continued.

"It's somewhere quiet where people can come if they need to rest or think or sort something out. Sometimes they come on their own for a short holiday; or we might have a group of people who want to have meetings without being interrupted."

"What sort of people?" asked Ashley.

"All sorts!" said Rachel. "There are sad people and tired people..."

"And a lot of people who just want a few day's peace and quiet," added her mother. "Anyone can come. We don't charge much and somehow there's always just enough money. We provide food and quiet and, in these lovely surroundings, God does the rest."

"Where are the ... guests now?" asked Ashley, looking around the living room. He was interested to see what these people looked like.

"The last one left this morning," Tessa replied. "We have new people arriving the day after tomorrow, so you can make as much noise as you like till then. But once they arrive, you'll need to remember to be quiet if you're anywhere near the front of the house. And, Rachel, remember to keep the Mole away from the side garden. Not everyone likes dogs, you know."

"But *everyone* loves Moley!" said Rachel, looking lovingly at the dog by her feet.

"Not everyone, darling," replied Tessa firmly.

"Why's he called the Mole?" asked Ashley.

"Well, because he's small and black," said Rachel.

"And because he has a habit of digging inconvenient holes all over the garden!" added Patrick, returning from wherever his thoughts had taken him. "Rachel, you must keep him out of the kitchen garden. Digby has threatened to bury him in one of his own holes if he digs up anything else!"

"And Mrs Latchett has mentioned paw marks again...," added Tessa.

19

"Poor Moley," sighed Rachel. "No one understands him, except me. Oh look, it's stopped raining! Can we go outside for a while?"

"Who's Digby?" asked Ashley as they left the house by the back door, with the Mole following.

"Digby does the garden and grows all the fruit and veg," Rachel explained. "No one knows if that's his real name, but he's been here years. He used to work for Uncle Leo."

They crossed a paved courtyard and followed a gravel path across a lawn towards a dark, neatly-clipped hedge that stretched the whole width of the garden. There was a small gap through which the path ran, turning into a flight of steps that led down to more grass at a lower level.

"Nice," said Ashley. "Like being in a park." He'd stopped to look at a stone lion that lay at the foot of the steps, its front paws stretched out. Rachel patted it affectionately.

"I used to sit on him when I was little," she said. "There are more around the place. The front door-knocker is one, and did you see there's one on each gatepost? Oh, and there's another on the sundial in the side garden, the one on the arch above the gate to the stables ... Uncle Leo liked lions. He called them his, um, namesakes."

"Namesakes?" Ashley looked puzzled.

"Yes," chuckled Rachel. "Because of him being called Leo, *you* know!"

"Leo?"

"Leo ... lion..."

"Oh ... I get it," said Ashley slowly. "Funny bloke, your uncle."

The rain began to fall again.

"Better go back," said Rachel reluctantly. "I'll show you the rest tomorrow. Did you bring a football? Mine's stuck in a tree. Come on, Moley-poley, race you back to the house!"

After unpacking and watching some TV, Ashley phoned his mum to tell her that he'd arrived. Later he lay in bed listening to the silence. He felt very strange. Every night he went to sleep with the hum of the city in his ears. Cars on the nearby main road, aircraft droning overhead, distant sirens hee-hawing to an emergency. It was all so familiar that he hadn't noticed it – until it stopped. Now the silence felt as loud as the traffic back home. It seemed to press into his ears until all he could hear was his own breathing. Straining his ears, he began to make out small sounds. There was water dripping somewhere outside the window. The wind in the trees sighed softly, like the gentle breathing of a giant animal. The house creaked. He leaned out of bed and rummaged in his backpack for his Walkman. Soon familiar music filled his head.

Staring drowsily at nothing in particular, he realised how far away he felt from his life at home. The quiet here was strange, but he was surprised to find that it didn't worry him.

I don't really know them and I've never been here before, but it feels very ... safe. Like I'm wrapped up in something soft and warm.

Jax and the Spookz seemed unreal. Cardboard cut-outs to be gathered up and put in a box at the back of a dark cupboard. He shut the door on them firmly.

I don't need to decide yet.

He sighed sleepily and hummed along quietly to the music.

21

"Ashley, are you asleep?" Tessa crept into the room. Ashley politely clicked the "off" button and slipped his headphones away from his ears.

"Just thought I'd pop up to say goodnight," she explained. "Are you comfortable?"

"Yes, thanks."

"Sure you've had enough to eat?"

Ashley thought about the colossal meal he'd eaten earlier that evening and smiled.

"I'm fine, thanks ... And I'm glad you didn't give it to the chickens." Tessa's eyes crinkled up as she laughed.

"Goodnight then, and sleep well."

He lay awake for a long time, straining to catch the tiny night-time sounds that occasionally broke the silence.

Will I ever get used to this?

Chapter 3

Ashley woke to the sound of a tractor grinding its way slowly along the lane. At first he was startled by his unfamiliar surroundings, and then he remembered where he was. Climbing out of bed, he padded over to the open window.

"Phew! It's *so* high!"

He looked down and down, and there was the Mole, busy digging at the far end of the lawn. A large, stooped figure in wellies trundled a squeaking wheelbarrow along a path and disappeared through a gateway in a tall brick wall. Ashley sniffed the air.

"Bacon!"

He felt hungry again, so he dressed quickly and hurried downstairs.

Sitting at the table eating his breakfast, he listened while Rachel told him her plans for the morning.

"First I'll show you the rest of the garden, then we could go up to the wood or..."

"Jobs first, please," said Tessa, coming across the passage from the kitchen with another pile of toast.

Rachel glanced up and sighed.

"OK."

Ashley looked at Rachel, about to ask a question. She grinned.

"We all have jobs to do," she explained. "Dad runs the office, does the shopping, helps Digby and collects guests from the station. Mum organises the house – cooking and cleaning, fixing things that break."

She paused to take another bite of toast and then continued, waving the slice as she spoke.

"Mrs Latchett comes in Monday to Friday to help Mum. She lives in the village and she used to work here when Uncle Leo lived here. If we're extra busy, her daughter Dawn helps too, when she's not running the playgroup in the village.

"So, what are your jobs then?" Ashley asked, carefully picking a shred of marmalade off his new T-shirt and rubbing at the sticky patch.

"Well, I look after Moley of course. Then I clear the table after meals, get things from the garden that Mrs Latchett needs for the meals and ... um, collect the eggs ... oh, and pick flowers to put in the bedrooms when new guests arrive. What else?" She screwed up her face as she tried to remember. "And in the holidays I help with the laundry. That's it really!" She leaned back in her chair and grinned again. Ashley was amazed.

"Don't you *mind*?" The idea of doing jobs was new to him. His mum had a cleaning lady who came once a week. And things like shopping and washing – well, they just sort of happened. Sometimes Mum grumbled about the state of his room, but she didn't seem to expect him to really *do* anything.

"Mind?" Rachel looked puzzled.

"Being made to do all that work. Doesn't sound fair to me. Like slavery or something."

"I *told* you," said Rachel. "We all have to help. There's no spare money to pay other people. Sometimes I get sick of it, but my jobs are OK ... Well, *most* of them. If you help, we'll do them quicker. Right, let's get this table cleared!"

Ashley was surprised to find himself stacking dirty dishes on a tray and following Rachel to the kitchen.

Mrs Latchett was a large, grey-haired woman, and today she wore a pink-striped apron as she stood at a big table in the middle of the room, calmly cracking eggs into a bowl. As Rachel and Ashley came in, she wiped her hands on her apron and picked up a piece of paper that lay on the table beside her.

"Morning, Mrs Latchett. This is Ash," Rachel announced. Mrs Latchett nodded and smiled.

"Hello, dear. Here's Digby's list and be careful with the eggs today. Some of yesterday's were only fit for scrambling!"

Rachel grinned. "Sorry. I was giving Moley a ride in the barrow and he must have sort of ... stood on them."

They hurried out the back door and into the courtyard.

"There's another one," said Ashley as they passed a small statue of a lion beside a water butt. This was a prancing lion, with its tail curved over its back.

"Told you," smiled Rachel, "They're all over the place!"

She raced off. Ashley followed more slowly, gazing about him.

It was a sparkling morning, noisy with bird-song. Each plant and blade of grass seemed to be coated

25

in diamonds as the early sun shone on wet leaves and petals.

It's all so clean, like it's just been washed.

"Oi, Ash! Come on!" He jogged after Rachel as she vanished through the gateway he'd seen from his bedroom window.

The vegetable garden was beside the stable yard. There were no horses in the stables now, and they were used to park cars and store tools. But the garden was still surrounded by its original high wall. It probably looked much the same as it had done two hundred years earlier when the house was new. It was criss-crossed by a grid of gravel paths that enclosed neat beds filled with rows of flowers and vegetables. Fruit trees grew along one wall. In the past a garden this big would have kept several men busy, but now there was only Digby. This was Digby's kingdom and they found him in his castle, the greenhouse.

"Digby, this is Ash. He's staying with us for a while," Rachel announced to the back of a large figure bent over a work bench. The shoulders moved a fraction but that was all.

"Ar," said a deep, gruff voice. "Sin 'im th's mornin', din't oy."

Rachel looked at Ashley and her eyebrows said, "When?"

He looked back and shrugged.

"But we've only just come out," said Rachel.

"At the winder, 'e wuz. Saw 'im."

"Oh, yeah, I was ... looking at the trees."

"Digby doesn't miss much, do you?" said Rachel. The shoulders twitched again as Digby turned around.

"See what matters," he grunted, inspecting Ashley carefully.

Ashley was startled. The large stooping figure and deep voice hadn't prepared him for the sight of a round pink face, innocent blue eyes, and wide rubbery mouth. Digby's ears stuck out and, underneath the tatty tweed cap, he was obviously totally bald. Ashley had the impression he was looking at an enormous baby. The contrast was confusing. Then Digby smiled – the widest, happiest, most welcoming smile that ever filled a human face – and Ashley relaxed.

"Hi, Digby," he said politely. Digby slowly stretched out an enormous, most unbaby-like hand, and they shook hands solemnly.

"Pleased to meet you, young 'un," he rumbled.

Help! I'm shaking hands with a gorilla!

Rachel was flapping Mrs Latchett's list at Digby.

"We've come for the veggies. We'll go and get the eggs and be back later." She whisked out of the greenhouse, and Digby and Ashley stared at the space where she had just been. Digby shook his head slowly.

"Tearin' rush, that young lady. Here 'n' there like one o' they blessed bumble bees, she is." His shoulders hunched in a quick, silent laugh as he turned back to the work bench. "Hens is down in the corner," he grunted, and he jerked his head towards the far corner of the garden.

Ashley wandered off and found Rachel in the hen run, holding a bucket and scattering grain in sweeping curves while the hens jostled and pecked around her feet. He stopped at the gate and peered through the wire mesh.

"Here, chook-chook-chook! Breakfast time! ... C'mon in, then!" she called to him. He didn't move.

Hmm, these things are bigger than you think when you see them close up. Pfwaagh, what a pong!

"It's OK, you know. They won't hurt you," she assured him. Ashley was annoyed.

I'm not scared ... really. It's just so messy. Yuk, there's chicken poo everywhere!

Reluctantly he creaked the gate open and stepped carefully through the feathery bodies. The hens took no notice of him as he followed Rachel into the shed at the back of the run.

"You hold the basket and I'll collect the eggs," said Rachel as she began feeling around in the straw of each nest box and bringing out the eggs.

"Want to do those over there?" She nodded towards the last two boxes. Ashley looked cautiously over his shoulder to check that none of the hens had decided to come back in, then he slipped his hand into the straw. His fingers closed around a smooth, warm egg.

"Hey, look at this one!" He held up an enormous dark-brown egg, so different from the ones that came cold from the fridge at home.

"Bet that's one of Gertie's," said Rachel. "She's that one over there. She's ever so old in hen years, but she still lays whopping eggs. Let's get the veg from Digby and then we can go up to the wood."

Later that morning they went into the wood that covered the hill beside the house. Ashley had changed into his old trainers after his visit to the hen run. Rachel wore a faded T-shirt, cut-off jeans and clumped along in battered wellies.

At school everyone wants the right trainers and things. She doesn't seem to care what she wears. I wonder why?

"Are we allowed up here?" Ashley asked.

"It's OK, because this land all belongs to the house," Rachel explained as they crossed the wooden bridge over the river.

"Does your mum let you come here by yourself?"

"Only as far as this bridge. I can't go into the wood on my own, in case I fall out of a tree or something!"

They stopped and leaned on the handrail, watching the muddy water as it surged under the bridge.

"It's usually clear and you can see the bottom." Rachel turned, Ashley following, and jogged up the steep, winding path between the towering tree trunks.

"All this as well as the garden?" said Ashley in amazement, thinking of the neat, professionally landscaped plot that surrounded his home. "Phew, it's some place!"

"Yes, well, Uncle Leo was quite rich, I suppose," admitted Rachel, "though he was very careful with money. He really loved Yaffle House and he wanted it to go to someone in the family who loved it too."

"Yaffle?"

"Oh, it's an old name for a green woodpecker. That's a *bird*," Rachel explained. "They make a sort of laughing noise that sounds like yaffle-yaffle. There are lots in the woods round here."

"What's that over there? A garage?" Ashley pointed to a small brick building in the wood below them. It had a low, domed roof and a door, but no windows, and there was ivy growing over its walls.

"That's the ice house," Rachel explained. "People used them in the old days to keep their food cold, before they had fridges."

"Can we get inside?" asked Ashley, interested. Rachel shook her head.

"It's all damp and dark, and it's a bit dangerous. The roof's starting to fall in."

They climbed on to the top of the hill and then stopped at a gap in the trees, turning to look out over the roof of the house to the farmland beyond. Ashley hadn't walked so far for a long time and he was panting. It was very quiet, apart from a sighing sound that the breeze made as it wandered through the tree-tops.

"It's like looking down on a huge map!" he puffed. "You can see all the roads and fields and things!"

A car, like a shiny dark-blue beetle, was crawling slowly along the lane that passed the house.

"Wow, a car!"

The first one I've seen since yesterday. I'd better make a note of that in my diary! "Saw a car today. Could this mean that we are not alone in this deserted land?"

"I suppose it's a bit quiet here for you," said Rachel. "I didn't like it when we first moved here, but I do now. You'll get used to it – guarantee it!"

There was a loud screeching sound and Ashley jumped.

"What was *that*?"

"Woodpecker," Rachel whispered. "Green one. There he goes!" She pointed as a large bird flew across to another tree and perched half-way up the trunk. It had a yellowish-green back and a bright splash of red on the top of its head.

"Big, isn't it?" breathed Ashley. "I didn't think we had birds with such bright colours in this country." Rachel nodded.

"There are *loads* of them up here in the woods. Like I said, that's how the house got its name," she stopped. "Where's Moley? I thought he was following us. Moleeeeey! Here, Moley!" She stuck two fingers into her mouth and gave a piercing whistle. Then they set off down the hill again as the Mole rocketed out of the bracken just ahead of them, eyes bright and tongue flapping like a piece of pink ribbon.

Just as they came out of the woods and were crossing the narrow wooden bridge, they saw the blue car again. It was parked in the lane beside the house

"Shh!" hissed Rachel, although Ashley hadn't spoken. "Get down here!" She dragged him down behind a bush and then, scooping the Mole into her arms, she hurried off, bent double, dodging from bush to tree until there was only the garden hedge between her and the road where the car stood. She turned and beckoned urgently.

"What's...?"

"Shh!"

Ashley shrugged and set off, trying to take cover as Rachel had done. The knees of his new jeans were muddy and wet by the time he reached her.

Yuk! This place is so messy!

The Mole was sitting panting beside her. He seemed to know that he had to be quiet.

"What's going on?" Ashley whispered.

"He's *spying!*" Rachel's voice was squeaky with indignation."

"Who's spying?"

"Old Pig Face!" Ashley looked at her uncertainly. *The girl's mad! She's been living in the country too long.*

At that moment there was the sound of a car door opening and, as they peered through the hedge, they could just make out a pair of legs in dark pin-striped trousers. The Mole growled quietly and Rachel tapped him sternly on his nose. There was a faint bleeping, then a smooth, confident-sounding voice spoke

"Tamara? Miles here. Just popped round to have another look at that property down Beech Lane. Have they had the report yet? Can you find out for me, my love?" There was a pause during which Rachel glared at the legs on the other side of the hedge and did vicious throat-cutting actions with her hand across her neck.

"Ya, still here," said the voice. "Uh-huh ... uh-huh ... Ya, I got it. *Bless* you, my love. Ya, it's got distinct possibilities. Uh-huh ... We'll give them a few days, then I think it'll be time to make a move. I'm sure they'll be ... cooperative. OK ... Ya, bye-ee!" There was another bleep and then the legs got back into the car and the door closed. As the engine started and the car moved off, Ashley found a larger hole in the hedge and caught a glimpse of a chubby-looking young man with fair wavy hair, pink complexion and a nose that definitely looked a bit like a snout.

Pig Face? Yeah!

He turned to Rachel. "So, what's going on? Who's that man and what's he doing here?"

Rachel stood up and turned back towards the

house. "It's lunch-time. I'll tell you on the way," and she marched off. Ashley hurried to join her.

"That's Mr Doubleby – Pig Face," said Rachel.

"The man you were talking about yesterday? The one you're worried about?"

Rachel nodded. "He's bought some farm cottages the other side of the village and is making them all posh and smart so he can sell them to rich people from big cities to use as holiday homes."

"What's wrong with that?"

"Well, he's got *loads* of money and was able to offer a really high price. No one else around here could afford to buy the cottages, so village people may have to move to town – and they don't want to. The primary school might have to close because there won't be enough children left, and we may lose the shop too. Soon there won't be any *real* village people living here and the houses will only have people in them at weekends and holidays, and it won't really be a proper village any more." She kicked at a clump of dandelions on the edge of the path and the seed heads exploded into a shower of twirling parachutes.

"But what did he mean about the property down Beech Lane?" asked Ashley. "Yaffle House is the only house down here..."

"Yes!" Rachel replied angrily. "Pig Face wants to buy Uncle Leo's house!"

"What for?"

Ashley was amazed at how quickly Rachel's mood had changed

"Oh, I don't know," she said crossly. "Make it into a fancy hotel or something, then charge people lots of money to stay!"

"Well, can't you just tell him to get lost?" suggested Ashley. Rachel shook her head.

"He's very determined. He started pestering Uncle Leo a few years ago."

"I bet Uncle Leo told him to push off!" said Ashley, thinking of the stern figure in the photograph. Rachel chuckled.

"He did! But now here he is again. He doesn't give up."

"But he can't *make* you sell the house to him, can he?" Ashley pointed out. Rachel shrugged her shoulders.

"Well, no," she said, uncertainly, "but Mum and Dad haven't got much money, and the house costs a lot to run, and there's big bills and things..."

"But you said Uncle Leo was rich."

"Well, he owned Yaffle House which is pretty big, and he left Dad some money to help. But, oh I don't know, it's all a bit complicated," she said. "Anyway, I wish that Doubleby bloke would just ... *disappear!*" They kicked off their shoes at the back door and went in for lunch.

Chapter 4

"Ee-yerk! He's splashing me!" Ashley stood unhappily on the river bank, while Rachel waded up to her knees in the water, tossing sticks for the Mole who was leaping and barking excitedly. There had been no more rain since Ashley had arrived at Yaffle House and the river had dropped to its usual level.

"Are you coming in, Ash? I thought we were going to try and build a dam?"

Ashley wasn't sure. He was getting used to living in the country, but he still didn't like the way things got messy. Today he had left all his smart clothes in the chest of drawers, and was wearing an old pair of shorts and a T-shirt that he wouldn't have been seen dead in at home. He looked at the water doubtfully.

Swimming pools I can cope with. You know the water's warm and clean. There might be bugs in here ... or things that bite your feet.

"Come *on!*" called Rachel, sloshing off downstream. "Here, Moley, fetch!"

Ashley reluctantly pulled off his trainers and socks, and picked his way down the bank. The water seemed clean enough and he couldn't see anything that looked like it might bite.

If I don't get in quick, she'll notice and start asking questions. Aargh, it's freezing! If that dog puts his dirty feet on me, I'll ... Hey, there's a fish!

Ashley was adjusting to life at Yaffle House. Many things seemed to be so different from what he was used to, but, almost from the start, he'd felt happy and comfortable. He liked Rachel and her parents and the old house. He had got used to saying a prayer before meals and helping with Rachel's jobs. Some things still puzzled him, though. He still didn't understand about the people who came to stay. Several new guests had arrived the previous morning. There had been a flurry of busy-ness after breakfast and then there had been the sound of cars arriving. He and Rachel had retreated to the back of the house, to keep out of the way. At one point he'd seen someone in the front hall – an ordinary middle-aged man with a suitcase. Later that day he and Rachel had seen him again as they passed the side garden on their way to the stable yard.

"Does Patrick know that bloke?" he asked, jerking his head in the direction of the man who sat reading in the sun on a garden seat. Rachel glanced over and shook her head.

"Don't think so, why?"

"Well, the way Patrick said hello, it was like ... like he was part of your family or a best friend ... like you were all really pleased to see him."

"Well, we *are* pleased to see him," said Rachel, looking surprised. "We want people to feel at home. That's why I put flowers in their rooms and Mrs Latchett makes loads of cakes and stuff."

"Even though they don't pay you much money?"

"Uh-huh."

"That's stupid."

"Stupid to be nice to people?"

"Well, everyone needs money," retorted Ashley defensively. "Patrick and Tessa do; you said so."

Rachel shrugged. "Yes, money's quite important sometimes, but it isn't the most important thing for Mum and Dad."

"What is, then?"

"Um," Rachel thought for a while. "*People* are, I suppose – looking after them, whoever they are. Not just being nice to ones who are rich and important."

"Hmph!" Ashley didn't know what to say after that, but he went on thinking and watching.

"Arf! Arf!" The Mole came paddling furiously towards the bank.

"Don't you dare come near me!" Ashley threatened as he waded carefully out into the middle of the river.

"Over here!" called Rachel.

Why am I doing this? Is this supposed to be fun?

"OK, I'm coming! The stones are slipp – oops – ery!" Ashley struggled over to join Rachel. She smiled.

"If you roll those two big rocks up from there, I'll try and fill in this gap with smaller stones," she suggested. They set to work on the dam. Before long, Ashley realised that his feet weren't cold and he hadn't been attacked by anything and that it didn't matter if you got a bit wet because the sun was so warm. They stopped to rest.

"Great!" said Ashley, wiping his hands down the back of his shorts.

"I wonder if we could build the dam *right* across the river?" Rachel said. "Then we could make a pool to swim in!"

"Flood the garden, most likely," said Ashley. The Mole lollopped towards them, making small tidal waves, but this time Ashley didn't worry. He bent down to pick up a stick and was about to throw it for the Mole when Rachel gasped.

"He's back!"

"Who?" Ashley paused, looking around, while the Mole paddled to and fro, watching the stick intently.

"Pig Face, who else?"

"Where?"

"In the lane again, a bit further down this time. I saw the car passing the gate."

Crouching and taking cover again, they made their way to the hedge by the lane. The Mole trotted happily beside them. Following along beside the hedge they soon saw, through the leaves, the glint of the dark-blue car parked at the bend, just before the ford. There was a battered pick-up beside it.

"He's got someone with him!" hissed Rachel. They parted the hedge carefully and peered through. Mr Doubleby was in the lane with an older, gloomy-looking man who stood with his shoulders hunched and hands stuck deep in his pockets.

"Who's the cheerful bloke?" whispered Ashley.

"Mr Mortimer ... builder,"

"What's..."

"Shh!"

The men were too far away to hear clearly, but scraps of conversation filtered through the hedge.

"Widen the gateway ... Car park there ... Knock down that wall..." Mr Doubleby waved his arms towards the garden.

"Don't like the look of that roof..." came Mr Mortimer's gloomy voice.

"Conservatory on the west wall..."

"There'll be damp, like as not..."

"Indoor swimming pool there..."

"Planning permission ... How soon?"

"Not long now ... only a matter of time..." Mr Doubleby smiled at the builder, smugly confident, as they strolled back down the lane. The sun still shone down on Yaffle House, he could feel it warm on his back, but Ashley shuddered.

Something dark and horrible is out in the lane, trying to get in here.

The car and truck drove slowly away to the main road. Rachel turned to Ashley.

"See what I mean? He just doesn't give up, does he?" She stared at the house. "He really thinks he's going to get it," she murmured in amazement.

"He can't *make* you," Ashley reminded her.

"No, he can't," she agreed. "Oh dear, I wish this wasn't happening!" She looked so forlorn, Ashley felt angry.

"Who does he think he is? He comes along, wanting to build car parks and knock things down. Can't he see what a mess it would be if he changed it all?"

"He wouldn't think it was a mess," Rachel sighed. "People like him don't really *see* things properly. They're so full up with their own ideas."

"Well, we'll have to make sure that his ideas don't happen!" said Ashley firmly. "You don't know it, Pig Face, but you're at war with us now and we're going to win!"

"Yes!" shouted Rachel, jumping up. "I don't

know how we'll do it, but we will!" They ran back through the sunshine towards the house.

There was no one in the living room, although the table was laid for the evening meal. Rachel went into the kitchen, where Mrs Latchett was lifting a tray of buns out of the oven.

"Where's everyone?"

"Well, m'dear, your mother was here not five minutes ago. She can't be far away." Rachel and Ashley stood in the passage.

"We could try and get the football out of the tree..." Rachel turned towards the back door, when the sound of voices from the office stopped her.

"Oh, Pat, this is *awful*. What're we going to *do*?"

Ashley stared at Rachel. Her face was grim.

What's happening? She's forgotten I'm here.

"I don't think we need to panic," said Patrick's voice quietly.

"Not panic?" Tessa sounded desperate. "It's been a struggle from the start, but we've always managed and we felt it was all so ... *right*. But now things like this keep happening. What'll we do?"

"Those people who arrived yesterday are the reason we're here," replied Patrick calmly. "We know this house has a special purpose, but we weren't promised that it would be easy. I know this is a bit hard to take, but we're not going to give up. I'm sure we can sort this out." There were nose-blowing noises.

"It's time to serve the meal." Tessa left the office and almost collided with Rachel and Ashley.

"Mum, what's happened?" asked Rachel anxiously. Tessa's eyes were red, but she was trying to smile.

"I must go and help Mrs Latchett." She hurried towards the kitchen.

"But, *Mum*...!"

Rachel and Ashley stood uncertainly in the study doorway. Patrick sat, leaning on Uncle Leo's big roll-top desk, his head in his hands. Hearing them, he turned, his face looking tired and strained.

"Dad, what's going on?" Rachel demanded.

"There's nothing to worry about," said Patrick gently.

Rachel folded her arms and looked sternly at her father.

"We're a team here," she said. "If there's something wrong, I *need* to know!"

Patrick sighed.

"OK, darling, this is the problem. Remember that Environmental Health man who came to inspect the kitchen last month? Well, here's his report." Patrick tapped some papers on the desk.

"What's wrong. Didn't he like our kitchen?" asked Rachel sharply.

"Oh, I think he *liked* our kitchen well enough; but he has to follow certain rules. When you're cooking food for people in a hotel or such-like, there have to be high standards of cleanliness."

Rachel was furious. "But Mrs Latchett is *very* clean!"

"Mrs Latchett's not the problem," said Patrick. "It's the kitchen itself. He says, amongst other things, that we must redecorate completely, replace the floor tiles and some of the work-tops, and get a new fridge and freezer."

"Phew!" whistled Rachel. "That'll cost a lot."

"Yes, it's much worse than we expected," her

41

father agreed. "And, as you know, we were hoping to replace the central-heating boiler before next winter – so, yes, it's going to cost a lot of money." He ran his fingers through his wispy hair as he continued. "Then that chap Doubleby turned up again today. It's no wonder Mum's a bit upset. Funny he should arrive just now. Makes you wonder how much he knows..."

Ashley stood in the background, watching. He was impressed with the way Patrick spoke to Rachel. Ashley's parents never let him in on adult conversations and he had no idea how much things cost, apart from what he bought with his own pocket money.

They really are a team – not a grown-up talking to a kid. And they're very worried about this. At home, when the dishwasher broke, it wasn't a big problem – Mum just went and bought another one. And it didn't take long to decide we'd get cable TV. Mum and Dad sometimes grumble a bit about prices, but no one seems really worried. This is different, though.

Ashley wanted to be helpful.

"Couldn't you put your prices up a bit?" he suggested.

Patrick smiled at Ashley, but shook his head. "That's an idea, Ashley. But, you see, this isn't like an ordinary hotel. The sort of people who come here sometimes can't afford high prices. We don't want lack of money to stop people who need to be here from coming, so we keep the prices low."

"Sometimes people just pay what they can manage," added Rachel.

"Until now we've been able to make enough

money to keep going, but big bills like these are very difficult to pay," explained Patrick.

"What happens if we can't do the kitchen?" asked Rachel, staring very hard at her father.

"If we don't do the work within a certain time, we'll have to close. It's the law," he added quickly as he saw Rachel open her mouth to speak.

"What're we going to do?"

"Well, first of all, we're *not* going to panic," said Patrick. "I'm sure God knows what's going on. We need to ask him to show us what to do." He stood up and stretched. Then he tousled Rachel's hair. "Come on, let's go and eat."

"We saw Mr Doubleby in the lane this afternoon," said Rachel during the evening meal. Ashley saw Tessa shoot a look at Patrick.

"Yes," said Tessa, "he called while Dad was out, wanting to know if we'd considered his offer."

"You said no, didn't you?" demanded Rachel fiercely.

"Of course I did! Dad and I make decisions together, you know that,"

"But you don't need to decide *anything!*" Rachel fumed. "He's not having Uncle Leo's house, he's not!" Ashley watched as Rachel's eyes filled with tears.

This is serious.

"Calm down, Rachel," said Patrick quietly. "Uncle Leo wanted his house to stay in the family and we're going to make sure it does. I admit that our finances are a bit shaky at the moment, but we'll manage. Yaffle House is a very special place, and so many people have been helped by staying here that I don't believe God wants it to get into the hands of a chap like Doubleby." Ashley listened, interested.

He's talking about God again. He really seems to think that God can help.

"Of course, you know what would solve our problem, don't you?" Tessa said as she passed Patrick another mug of tea. Patrick stared into space, head poked forward, frowning slightly.

"Not that treasure business again?"

"Yes! Uncle Leo's famous Missing Loot!" said Rachel.

Patrick smiled fondly at Rachel.

"Perhaps you should start looking for it," he suggested. "Then you wouldn't have time to worry."

Chapter 5

"Here, take these." Rachel handed an untidy bunch of flowers to Ashley. "Now, come and help me put them in water. The new guests arrive this morning."

Ashley stuffed them into the basket he was holding. Nearly a day had passed since they had seen Mr Doubleby out in the lane again and Ashley had a question buzzing inside his head.

"This loot – is it real or what?"

"I *think* so," Rachel replied as she filled some vases with water and began to sort the flowers.

"Why is it missing?"

"Well, there's this story ... Here, you put a few of each colour into these, OK?" Ashley obeyed, clumsily poking flowers into the vases as Rachel talked.

"You know the Second World War?"

"Mm, we did it at school last term."

"Yes, so did we. Anyway, some people thought that Hitler might win and ... Don't cram them in like that, you're squashing them!"

"OK, OK, I've never done this before, have I?"

What would Jax say if he saw me now?

"Sorry. Well, anyway, I don't know if Uncle Leo thought that Hitler would win. Maybe he just wanted to be careful, so he hid some of his valuable things to keep them safe."

"What sort of things?" Ashley's mind saw pictures of treasure chests.

"We're not sure, but Dad thinks it would be something small enough to hide easily, like money or jewellery."

"Well, the war was ages ago," Ashley pointed out. "Where's the loot now?"

"Dunno," replied Rachel, shrugging her shoulders.

"Didn't anyone ask him about it?"

"Don't think so. You see, you just couldn't be nosy with Uncle Leo."

"And now he's dead and you *can't* ask him," said Ashley, exasperated. "Didn't anyone try to find it?"

"Dad did. When he was a boy he used to come on holiday here. He spent hours digging holes. Once he got into *big* trouble for pulling up some floor boards!"

Ashley tried to imagine Patrick being a naughty little boy.

"There! All finished," Rachel announced briskly.

"Now let's go over to the stables and look for a cricket bat," said Ashley. "Patrick thinks there's one in the loft."

"But I thought we were going to start looking for the loot," replied Rachel.

"Are you serious?" Ashley laughed. But, looking at Rachel, he realised that she was.

"We *are* going to look for it, aren't we?" she challenged.

"*If* it exists," Ashley shrugged.

"I'm sure it does," Rachel insisted. "Anyway, it's worth trying."

"OK, what'll we do?"

"What we need first is a clue to get us started,"

said Rachel. "Uncle Leo liked riddles and hard crosswords. I think he wanted someone to find his treasure, but it had to be the *right* person and he didn't want to make it too easy."

"Well, he must have written something down," said Ashley. "*I* would. Just to make sure I didn't forget."

"You mean a rolled-up map with a big X to mark the place?" Rachel teased. Ashley was annoyed.

"No, just a bit of paper hidden at the back of a drawer or in a secret compartment or something."

"Dad uses Uncle Leo's old desk in the office. We could have a look in there," Rachel suggested, scrambling up.

As they came into the house, they could hear Patrick talking on the phone in the office. They fidgeted impatiently by the back door, and at last there was a gentle rumble as the chair rolled back and then Patrick appeared in the office doorway.

"Ah, there you are," he said. "I'm going over to Harpole's farm in a minute to borrow their chainsaw. I need to cut up that dead tree for firewood. Want to come?"

Rachel looked at Ashley. He shrugged and nodded.

"Yeah, OK, but..."

"But we've got something important to do first," Rachel interrupted. "We'll be along in a minute."

"I'll be leaving in fifteen minutes and not a moment later."

As soon as Patrick had gone out, Rachel and Ashley hurried into the office where they stood staring at the old desk.

"Well," said Rachel. "Here it is. Where do we start? There are so many little shelves and drawers!"

The desk was far too heavy to move out from the wall, so they had to make do with searching the front and the sides for secret drawers or a trigger to open a hidden compartment. Rachel gave up quickly, but Ashley continued to search carefully while she began inside the desk.

"We've *got* to find a clue, *quick!*" she muttered as she scrabbled about impatiently, trying not to disturb Patrick's books and papers.

"If we're going to the farm we need to get moving," said Ashley some time later, glancing at his watch.

"Might as well," sighed Rachel. "What a waste of time! We haven't found anything here."

After the trip to Harpole's farm and then an hour of helping to stack the wood that Patrick cut, they had tea and rock cakes out in the sunny courtyard. Then, when Patrick went back to work, Tessa sat on in the sunshine with a second mug of tea. She was calm and smiling once more.

"Mum, what'll happen if we have to stop having guests?" asked Rachel. "Would we have to leave Yaffle House?"

Tessa sipped slowly and thoughtfully. "Maybe," she said eventually. "Dad would need to get another job. So would I, and you know how hard it is to find work round here. We certainly couldn't afford to stay, with all the work that needs doing on the house."

"So we'd have to sell?" Rachel said quietly. Tessa nodded

"And Pig Face would buy it!" choked Rachel through gritted teeth. "There's no way Uncle Leo would let his house go to someone like that. He just wouldn't!"

"Rachel, that's no way to talk about Mr Doubleby." Tessa frowned. "But I agree; Uncle Leo was a shrewd man. I'm sure he knew this sort of thing might happen and he made provision. He just didn't do things like ordinary people do – it wasn't his style."

"You mean that letter he wrote to Dad, just before he died?" said Rachel.

"Yes, it was a bit mysterious, but it was probably just Uncle Leo's way of saying goodbye to someone he was very fond of," said Tessa.

Rachel sat up, bright and alert.

"Can I show Ash the letter?"

"Sure," said Tessa, "Half a mo' and I'll get it."

"Be gentle with it," she warned as she handed it to Ashley. "It's very special."

Carefully he unfolded the single sheet of paper and read.

"My dear Patrick,

Not much time left now. I shall be leaving shortly, I think. Once the worthy Mr Arbuthnot has sorted out my affairs, you will receive the keys to the house and all necessary papers. I know you will love it and continue to use it in the way that I have.

I believe there has been idle talk, from time to time, regarding my 'loot'. When first it was concealed, my plan was purely to confound that fiend and his unspeakable hordes. Later, it seemed best that it should remain hidden until such time as it was needed. When that time comes, all will be made clear. In the meantime, I shall be watching over you: a benevolent presence within my beloved home.

So, my dear boy, this is 'au revoir' and not 'good-bye', for I have absolutely no doubt that we shall be reunited one day.

God bless you,

Your affectionate Uncle Leo."

"That's it?" asked Ashley.

Rachel nodded.

"It's a bit ... sort of ... weird, isn't it?"

"He was very ill at the time," Tessa explained. "His mind may have been confused."

"No, he was just being Uncle Leo," said Rachel. "You know how he enjoyed a joke. I think this is just another of his puzzles. He used to say, 'Use your brain, child!', didn't he?"

Tessa smiled.

"OK then, you two had better start using your brains."

Rachel looked at Ashley. He looked back and shrugged.

So, all we've got to do is to find some treasure, which may not even exist and was hidden by a nutty bloke over fifty years ago. Shouldn't be too hard, should it!

"I know they're in here *somewhere!*"

Later that afternoon, Ashley was sitting on the floor in Rachel's room, playing on his Game Boy. He'd hardly touched it since he arrived at Yaffle House. Rachel had tried it, but hadn't been impressed. "What, you just have to keep zapping things?" she'd asked in disbelief. "Not much fun," she'd decided after five minutes. Now she was rummaging in a drawer, looking for tennis balls to use with the cricket bat they'd found.

Ashley looked up and gazed thoughtfully at the photograph of Uncle Leo. The old gentleman stared back at him. Was it just the light reflecting off the glass, or were the eyes sparkling with mischief?

I'm starting to imagine things now!

"Was that what he meant when he said he'd be watching over you?" he said, pointing at the photograph. Rachel stopped searching and looked up at Uncle Leo's picture.

"Maybe," she replied. "He gave it to me and asked me to look after it. Having it here makes me feel as though he's still sort of with us."

Ashley went on staring at the photograph. A stern voice seemed to be whispering in his head. "Use your brain, child, use your brain..."

"Can you get it down off the wall?" he asked suddenly. Rachel looked doubtful.

"It's very heavy. You'll have to help. Why?"

"Not sure," replied Ashley tensely. "I just think we need to, OK?"

Rachel didn't argue, and together they stood on the bed and carefully unhooked the heavy old frame from the wall, swaying to keep their balance. Laying it on the bed, they climbed down and studied it closely. The moustache and eyebrows seemed to bristle even more fiercely, but the eyes were warm and friendly.

"Help me turn it over," said Ashley. Rachel looked puzzled.

The back of the frame was covered with thick cardboard and stuck down with brown paper tape. There was nothing to see but a label with the name and address of the picture framer.

"What are you looking for?" asked Rachel.

"There's something funny about the back," Ashley replied. "Not sure what. Just looks wrong."

They sat for a while, then Rachel ran her finger along the tape on the bottom edge.

"This is a different brown from the rest," she suggested.

"That's it!" said Ashley with satisfaction. He looked more closely. "This bit's newer. It's been stuck on more recently."

Rachel leapt to her desk and found a pair of scissors.

"Quick! Let's see if we can slit it open!"

"Careful!" Ashley warned. "Don't go slicing up something important!"

Rachel ran one blade of the scissors along the paper tape, just at the point where the cardboard fitted into the frame.

"Look, the cardboard's a bit loose, I can get my finger in underneath ... *just*," said Rachel breathlessly. Ashley clenched his fists with excitement.

More cautious wriggling with her finger and Rachel gasped. "Yes!"

"What is it?"

"I've got it ... It's coming ... There!" She held up a piece of folded, yellowing paper. "Look! It was tucked in just behind the cardboard."

They both bent over the paper as Rachel unfolded it.

"It's a poem!" snorted Ashley in disgust.

"No," Rachel replied slowly as her eyes scanned the page. "I think it's one of Uncle Leo's puzzles. Listen.

"The time has come to seek what now you need,
   It has lain protected, safe from others' greed.
   But now, you who know and love each corner of this place
   And strive to keep the purpose others would erase,
   Take heart! The final quest is now begun.
   It may take work but also will be fun.
   The prize will surely be worth all the seeking,
   For then this happy spot will be forever in safe-keeping.

   "A namesake faces south,
   Where another empties his mouth."

Ashley quickly reread the lines himself and then looked at Rachel. "Looks like a poem to me."

The bloke must have been completely loony. Fancy writing bits of poetry and sticking them inside pictures! What's wrong with giving people a cheque or a big pile of money? Why poetry and puzzles? Honestly!

"It *is* a poem, but look," said Rachel earnestly. "It's about us – people who love the house being in trouble and finding something that'll help – and things being all right in the end."

Ashley looked doubtful.

You can understand why she wants to believe all this stuff. She's desperate. But what use is a bit of poetry?

"Well, what do we do next?" he challenged her.

"I'm not sure," she admitted. "But I think there's a clue in here somewhere. We need to use our brains!" Ashley smiled.

"OK then. Let's get to work."

Rachel nodded and they heaved the heavy frame back on to the wall. Before jumping down off the bed, Rachel turned back and blew a kiss.

"Thanks, Uncle Leo," she said.

Chapter 6

It was dark. Very dark. Ashley could see nothing, but he knew he was inside somewhere cramped. He was unhappy; maybe a bit scared. Once, when he was a little boy, he'd accidentally got shut in a cupboard. He had known there was sunlight and life outside the door, but he'd been shut in the dark and couldn't reach them.

There were people here with him now in the dark.

"Got to get away from them," he muttered. He groped around in the blackness, stumbling forward, his breathing sounding loud and hoarse in his ears. The people were still there, he knew they were, moving slowly and silently through the darkness towards him.

"Got to get out!" he whimpered in panic. His hands touched a wall. He began to feel his way along it. There *must* be a door!

Suddenly the surface changed; he felt planks of rough wood. His hand knocked against cold metal. A door handle.

"Now I can get out!" he sighed with relief. But as his hands gripped the door handle, a sound broke the silence around him.

Knocking. Someone was knocking on the door. Outside there was someone trying to get in!

Panic clutched at his stomach.

"What can I do? If I stay here they'll get me, but if I open the door...?"

Ashley stood frozen and undecided while the knocking continued.

"Ash! Wake *up!*" Rachel burst into the room. Ashley squinted at her and tried to look as though he was awake.

"Uh?"

"Are you OK?"

Ashley blinked a few times and nodded. "Yeah."

"Good, 'cause it's time you were up. Mrs Latchett needs a few bits from Digby, then we're going to work out the first clue, aren't we?"

How can she be so cheerful this early in the morning? Look at the time! Doesn't she ever sleep?

"Uh-huh."

Rachel whisked away and Ashley groaned to himself as he crawled out of bed. It took a while for the feelings in the dream to leave him. He reached automatically for his headphones, fumbled in his back-pack for a different tape and then sighed with relief as the music in his head replaced the dark fears. The memory of the dream and its power to frighten him faded as the sun shone brighter.

"Mrs Latchett says can she have more carrots today?" Ashley and Rachel were standing in Digby's greenhouse.

"Need me fork," grunted Digby. Rachel and Ashley followed him to the carrot bed and watched while he gently loosened the soil around the carrots and pulled them out.

"Digby," said Rachel casually, "you know Uncle Leo's missing loot?"

"Told you before," Digby growled as he shook the loose earth from the carrots and laid them in the barrow.

"I know you did, Digby," Rachel said hastily, "but I just wondered if there was anything else you needed to tell me. You know, something that perhaps you'd forgotten?" Digby turned slowly towards them with an earnest expression in his pale blue eyes.

"Mister Leo wanted things kept safe, 'e did. Till they wuz needed, 'e said."

"I know, Digby – that's all he ever seems to have said to anybody. But you were here in the war, weren't you? Can't you remember *anything*?"

"Only a lad then, wurn't oi?" Digby replied, turning back to the carrots. Rachel looked helplessly at Ashley.

Either this bloke's nuts too or he's just not telling. I'll have a go.

"Digby," Ashley began, "we've got something that might help us to find it." He looked at Rachel and she nodded. "You see, we've found this and we think it might be a clue."

Rachel held out Uncle Leo's poem and Digby took it, after carefully wiping his hands on his trousers. He read slowly, his lips moving silently.

"Humph!" he grunted. "Were a rare 'and at rhymes, wuz Mister Leo."

"Yes, but what do you think it *means*?" persisted Rachel.

Digby slowly reread the lines at the bottom of the page, then his shoulders shook with silent laughter.

"Liked 'is jokes, did Mister Leo."

Ashley and Rachel exchanged more helpless glances. Digby looked at them and grinned.

"Namesake," said Digby deliberately. "His namesake."

Ashley stared at Rachel and saw her slowly start to understand.

"Namesake...? *His* namesake! Yes! Brilliant!" She leapt into the carrot patch and hugged Digby. "Of course, I should have spotted that straight away!" She turned to Ashley, who was looking puzzled.

"Namesake, get it?"

"No."

"Name. What was his *name*?"

"Leo..."

"And what does *leo* mean?"

"Lion. You said so the other day. LION! Ooh!" Rachel laughed with delight.

"But which lion, and *where*?" Ashley felt things were still far from clear.

"Think about it," said Rachel. "What has Uncle Leo put all around the garden?"

At last he understood.

"So you reckon this has got something to do with one of the lions in the garden?"

"Yes, it's got to be! Come on!" Rachel was already on her way.

"Carrots!" said Digby solemnly. Gravel spurted up as Rachel skidded to a halt.

At last the barrow was piled high and they were able to go.

"Oh, Digby," said Rachel. "Do you think you could keep this a secret? We don't want anyone else to know yet. OK?" She beamed at him.

"Humph!"

As they turned to go, Digby spoke again. "Round here somewhere, oi'm sure o' that. Just wanted to make sure the roight folks found it, din't 'e?"

I hope you're right, Digby old mate, because otherwise we're going to be wasting a lot of time!

"Right, now what?"

Ashley and Rachel stood at the front door, staring at the big brass lion's-head knocker. Rachel clutched Uncle Leo's poem and read aloud.

"One namesake, faces south ... Where's south?"

"We need a compass," said Ashley.

"Haven't got one," said Rachel. "There must be another way to work it out."

"Well," said Ashley, staring around him, "I know the sun rises in the east and sets in the west. It comes in my bedroom window in the morning so that must be east." He was sounding a lot more confident than he felt.

"Naughty Elephants Squirt Water!" said Rachel suddenly.

"Uh?"

"It's a way of remembering the compass points," she explained, spinning around on the spot and pointing as she spoke.

"So, if your window faces east ... Naughty Elephants Squirt ... right, this is south!" said Rachel triumphantly, pointing towards the house. They looked at the knocker and shook their heads.

"This isn't the one," said Rachel. "He's facing away from the house. Bother!"

"Better try one of the others then," Ashley suggested.

"OK, we'll go to the side garden and look at the one on the sundial." But that one faced west, and the one by the water butt faced east.

"We're running out of lions!" said Rachel as they ran along the path behind the house. "We'll try the one by the steps next."

Stopping at the top of the steps, Rachel did her Human Compass act again. Muttering to herself and stabbing the air with a finger, she stopped at the word 'squirt' and slowly looked down at the stone lion crouching at the bottom of the steps.

"He's facing south!" she yelled, leaping down the steps. "He must be the one in the clue!"

Oh yeah? I must be mad to be doing this. It's like a crazy treasure hunt!

Ashley joined Rachel beside the lion. He picked at a patch of yellow lichen on its back and looked out across the garden, following the gaze of the stone eyes.

"What's he looking at?" he asked. "It's a pity he can't tell us."

"A namesake faces south ... where another empties his mouth," Rachel chanted slowly. "Another what?"

"Namesake, I suppose," said Ashley. "You know where all the lions are. Is there one down there?"

Rachel looked thoughtful. "There's the one on top of the stables gateway, and there's the knocker and the painting in the office, and the one by the water butt..." She looked apologetic. "I don't think there are any in that part of the garden."

"All we can do then is walk in a straight line from *this* lion and see what we come to," said Ashley, feeling that someone needed to make a decision.

Walking side by side, and looking over their shoulders now and then to make sure they were still in line with the lion's gaze, Rachel and Ashley crossed the lower lawn and walked towards the high back wall of the garden. Creeping plants trailed from the old wall and almost covered a small pond. It curved out from the wall like a capital D and was edged with moss-covered stones.

"We'll need a ladder to go any further," said Ashley, checking again over his shoulder.

"Let's have a good look here first," Rachel replied. "Perhaps there's another lion nearby."

"Well, I'm not looking in *that!*" said Ashley firmly, jerking his head at the ink-black water of the pond. He looked down at the scuffed toes of his trainers.

Why does everything in the country have to be so messy? It took me weeks to get Mum to buy me these.

Rachel wasn't listening. She was scrabbling along the wall, pulling the plants aside. Ashley shrugged and started to do the same on the other side of the pond. Spiders and dead leaves showered down on them.

"Yuk!" he shuddered, flicking off something that scuttled up his arm.

"What is it?"

"Don't know. Something with a lot of legs!"

"Careful it doesn't fall in the pond. It may not be able to swim."

Ashley looked at her in disbelief, but she wasn't joking.

Great! I'm ruining my clothes and being attacked by enormous insects, and she's worried about them getting wet! She's as nutty as her crazy uncle!

Gritting his teeth, he continued to search along the wall, leaning further out over the pond.

"This is a waste of time. There's nothing..." His fingers had touched something that wasn't brick wall.

"What?"

"There's something on the wall, under all this stuff, but I can't reach it."

"Lean out a bit more," said Rachel, hopping with impatience.

"I *can't!*"

"You're not trying!"

"Look, if I wanted to drown myself, I'd choose a nice, clean swimming pool!" They glared at each other.

"Your arms aren't long enough!" snapped Rachel.

"OK, you do it then, Ape Woman!" Ashley snarled back. They stood, breathing heavily for a few moments, then Rachel smiled.

"Sorry, Ash, but this is so important."

Ashley shrugged and smiled back. "It's OK, I shouldn't have yelled either."

What am I saying? The Spookz don't apologise ... ever! Funny her being so quick to say sorry, though.

"We need a bit of wood – something we can use like a bridge across the pond," suggested Ashley.

"Yes," Rachel agreed. "There'll be something in the stables."

"Raaaay-chel!" A distant voice called from near the house. Rachel gasped and clapped her hand over her mouth.

Chapter 7

"Oh no! I promised Mum I'd go over to Askew's store this morning. Mrs Askew's lending her some books about keeping chickens." She glanced at her watch. "We've got time to do it before lunch if we go now."

Tessa was standing on the path at the top of the steps as they hurried across the lower lawn towards her.

"What on earth are you doing down there?" she asked as they panted up the steps.

"Sorry, Mum, I forgot about your books. We'll go now," gasped Rachel, ignoring the question.

"That's fine," Tessa replied. "Can you get a large bag of self-raising flour and a book of second class stamps, too?"

"OK, we're on our way!" Rachel whirled past and was off at top speed. Ashley grinned shyly at Tessa. She smiled back with a look of pretend exhaustion.

"Here's the bag and the money. She won't realise she needs them till you're halfway there. Better hurry or she'll leave you behind, too!"

"I'm not riding *that!*" Ashley stood in the stable yard, staring in horror at the old bike.

"Why not?" asked Rachel, surprised.

"It's ... it's ... old."

"So?"

"It probably doesn't work."

"It does. Dad fixed it. It goes really well."

"But it's all ... high up," he protested. "And it's got funny handlebars!"

"But it *goes*," Rachel pointed out calmly. "That's what matters."

Ashley thought of the eighteen-speed mountain bike he'd got for Christmas, then looked at the old bike and cringed.

"I know, I know!" he muttered fiercely. "It's just so *embarrassing!*"

"Look, don't worry," said Rachel. "The road to the shop is very quiet. We'll hardly see anyone, unless," she giggled, "unless you count Mr Harpole's cows!"

Ashley sighed and took the bike.

I can't believe this is happening. Please don't let anyone back home hear about this!

Rachel stuffed the shopping bag into the basket on her own battered bike, then leapt on.

"We'll go there on the road," she called over her shoulder. "Then we can come back along the lane and get wet in the ford."

At the gate they turned right into Beech Lane. Then they were off, heads down, knees pumping, up to the junction with the main road.

Clunk-tick, clunk-tick. Ashley's bike was making some very strange noises. Rachel was right, though – it went really well. By the time they reached Askew's store he was beginning to enjoy himself. True, the bike looked like something from a museum. But once you'd got used to being so high up, it was fun. He could see over the hedges, and the big wheels ate up the distance.

"Phew, I'm out of practice," he gasped as they arrived at the shop and dropped their bikes in the hedge. "Is this it, then?" he continued, looking at the small shop with its cluttered windows.

There was nothing smart about Askew's store, but it provided all the basic things that the locals needed, including a chance for a good gossip.

How do people manage without proper shops? What would me and my friends do at weekends with no shopping mall to hang around in?

Inside the shop Mrs Askew was chatting to an elderly man as she packed his shopping bag. Rachel found the flour and then they waited by the post office counter. Ashley was reading the headlines on the newspapers in the rack on the wall, when suddenly Rachel jabbed him in the ribs.

"Wha...?"

She put a finger to her lips and jerked her head towards the two figures still talking by the till.

"Well, Robbie, if what you say is true, it's the worst bit of news we've had for a long time," sighed Mrs Askew sadly.

"Ah, 'tis true enough m'dear," insisted old Robbie. "I had it from Agnes Harpole herself. She says he told her he's got 'big plans for the area' and we all know what *that* means!"

"We mustn't jump to conclusions, just because he bought the farm cottages over on the by-pass," insisted Mrs Askew.

"Huh!" grunted Robbie, "I tell you, that type always get what they're after. He's been wavin' his cheque book at Harpole for weeks now, making him 'generous offers'. How long're he and his missis going to hold out? They're not getting any younger. The money would be useful."

"But there's been Harpoles on that land since the Domesday Book!" Mrs Askew protested.

"Ah well, maybe there has. But I'm telling you there are big changes coming." Robbie nodded gloomily. "If we can't raise the money to repair the roof on the Village Hall, we won't be using *that* no more neither, and you can be sure he'll be buying that an' all!"

"We need the Hall!" said Mrs Askew. "What about the playgroup and all the other folks who use it?"

Robbie sighed. "T'ain't the village I used to know. He's got plans alright. Just look at the way he's houndin' the Butterworths over at Yaffles..."

Mrs Askew shushed Robbie and glanced at Rachel and Ashley standing in the far corner of the shop, pretending they hadn't heard.

Old Robbie picked up his bag and clumped out of the shop while Mrs Askew bustled up, smiling and chatting about the weather. When they'd paid for their shopping, she went out the back to find the books for Tessa.

"Pig Face again," said Ashley quietly.

"I knew he was up to something," muttered Rachel. "Him and his money and his Big Plans!"

She looked so desperate, Ashley wanted to cheer her up. "At least we've started looking for the loot," he said.

"Yes, but things aren't happening very fast, are they? We need to do something quick, before he takes over the whole area," she said.

"When we get back, we're going to get that plank

and check the wall by the pond," Ashley reminded her, mainly because he couldn't think of anything else to say.

Rachel flashed him a smile. "Thanks, Ash. I'm glad you're here to help."

Help? How can I really help? It's all so hopeless I don't reckon there's anything we can do ... apart from rob a bank, maybe!

Carrying the books and shopping, they stepped out into the sunshine and collected their bikes. Rachel seemed to be feeling better.

"Anyway," she said as she untangled her handlebars from the hedge, "we're not going to give up, are we?" Ashley heaved his old machine upright and flicked a green caterpillar off the saddle.

"Nope. Pig Face doesn't realise who he's up against," he agreed.

Later, during lunch, the phone rang. Patrick was still outside mending the lawnmower.

"I'll go," said Tessa. Rachel and Ashley continued eating. Ashley was more tired from the cycle ride than he wanted to admit. After three cheese scones he was feeling a bit better, but already his legs were starting to ache.

Why are things so far apart in the country? At home I can get to town easily. It's very tiring living here!

Tessa came back into the room and slumped down heavily into her chair. Her face was red and she looked flustered.

"What's the matter?" Rachel asked sharply.

Tessa sighed deeply. "I think I've just done a rather silly thing. That was Mr Doubleby. He wants to come and look over the house."

"He can't!" protested Rachel. "It's not for sale. You said no, didn't you?" She stared at her mother in disbelief. "You *didn't*...? Oh, *Mum*!"

"Darling, he's so persuasive – and he didn't seem to hear me saying no," Tessa explained helplessly. "I tried, honestly, but short of being really rude..."

"When's he coming?" demanded Rachel.

"Next Tuesday afternoon."

"Well, we can phone and tell him we've changed our minds."

"Mm, yes, that's what we'll do," agreed Tessa, cheering up. "I need to check the laundry. Can you two clear the table before you go out?"

When she had gone, Ashley and Rachel sat staring at each other. "What do we do *now*?" sighed Rachel. "We're no nearer finding the treasure and now Pig Face is coming. We've *got* to stop him!" Ashley was only half listening as an idea took shape in his mind.

"I don't think we should try and stop him coming," he said slowly.

"But...!"

"He's so keen to come and snoop around, why not let him?"

"But, Ash...!"

"Listen! Even if you say no this time, he'll just try again. I think he should come and then we'll help him change his mind."

"How do we do that?"

"Has he ever been inside the house before? Does he know what it's like?"

"No."

"Well, what if he has such a *seriously* bad time in

here that he decides it's the last place he would ever, *ever* want to buy?"

Chapter 8

"You do it, Ash – you found it."

"You're lighter though. Maybe you should."

"OK, here goes!"

It hadn't taken long to find a plank amongst the clutter in the stables. Now they had laid it across the pond as near to the wall as they could get it. Cautiously Rachel stepped sideways onto the plank and edged along, holding the plants for support.

"You need to be in the middle. A bit further..."

"Ooo, the plank's bouncing," Rachel wobbled nervously. "Is this the right place?"

"Yes. Now what's under there?"

Rachel poked one arm through the tangle of leaves and began to feel along the wall behind.

"Brick ... brick ... still brick ..."

"Try lower down."

"No, it's just brick. Oh, here's something! Hang on while I get this stuff out of the way."

Together they managed to drag the leaves aside, then Ashley held them back while Rachel pulled a matted layer of dead stalks off the wall.

"You were right, Ash!" she gasped. "It's another of Uncle Leo's lions. Look!"

Peering out at them from the wall was a metal lion's face framed by a magnificent shaggy mane.

"I wonder why he was hidden under there?" said Ashley.

"I don't think he was meant to be hidden," said Rachel. "I think it's just that all this stuff has grown over him."

"Why put him there, though?" Ashley persisted. "Some of the lions around here *do* something as well as being ornaments, like the knocker and the sundial."

"I wonder if this one does something?" Rachel stared at the lion's head.

"What's in his mouth?" asked Ashley "I can't see properly from here."

Rachel peered and poked. "It's a pipe thing."

"What, you mean like he's smoking?" said Ashley.

Rachel laughed. "No! There's a piece of pipe inside his head that sticks out his mouth," she explained. "Wonder what it's for?"

"My arms are killing me. I'll have to let go for a bit," said Ashley. The plants swung back as Rachel scrambled along the plank.

"Well, we've found what the first lion was pointing at," she said, trying to sound encouraging.

"Yeah, but what now?" Ashley asked the obvious question.

"Perhaps we should give our brains a rest and think about something else for a while?" Rachel suggested. "How about plans for Pig Face's visit?"

Two hours later, after a lot of thinking and some arguments, Rachel and Ashley had made their plans. On a bit of paper in Ashley's pocket were two lists: things to be done and things they would need.

"Do you think we've got time?" wondered Rachel as they walked back to the house.

"Yeah, no problem!" replied Ashley cheerfully.

"What if there's trouble?" said Rachel. "I don't mind about me, but you don't need to be involved in this. It's not really your problem."

Ashley thought for a moment. "But I *want* to be in it. This place is happy and full of ... light. I don't want it to be spoiled," he said awkwardly. "Anyway, I don't like Pig Face. He pushes people around and I don't like bullies."

Rachel was grateful. "Thanks, Ash. I think Uncle Leo would be on our side, too."

Ashley thought about the lists and nodded. "I think he'd be really pleased," he said. "Probably give us a few ideas of his own!"

The morning sun shone out of a cloudless sky. Already the dew had gone from the grass, and the leaves hung limply on the trees. Rachel and Ashley had woken early, feeling hot. The attic rooms never really cooled down at night in this sort of weather. They had eaten breakfast and fed the Mole, and now they were watching TV.

"Mornin' all! Looks like another scorcher," called Mrs Latchett, arriving through the back door. "My Len was out half the evenin' watering his garden – it's *that* dry!" She disappeared into the kitchen and then came back, wearing her apron and waving a piece of paper. "You two ready then? Here's the list. Now, try and persuade that Digby to let us have some more raspberries for dessert. I know he's got plenty; the old rascal was boasting about them to my Len in the Queen's Head the other night."

"He wants you to make jam," said Rachel.

"Well, you just tell him to send me over a nice boxful and I'll see what I can do."

Ashley and Rachel collected the wheelbarrow and trundled it over to the kitchen garden. They were both thinking about the lion's head they had found.

"I wonder if we need to try Digby again?" said Rachel, opening the gate for Ashley to wheel the barrow through. "He knew Uncle Leo the longest of anybody that's alive now."

They found Digby in his greenhouse, having a snack and reading the newspaper. He sat in a rickety old armchair, eating a gigantic sandwich that had bits of bacon dangling out of the sides. He nodded and went on chewing steadily.

"Digby, we need your help again," said Rachel, settling herself comfortably on a sack of compost.

"Ar," Digby replied.

"It's about the loot," Ashley explained.

"Ar."

"We've solved part of the first clue, but, well, we're a bit stuck," Rachel explained. Digby took another enormous bite of sandwich.

"Show him the clue again, Ray," prompted Ashley. Digby carefully laid down the remains of the sandwich on his newspaper and took the crumpled paper from Rachel.

"We're sure we've found which namesake faces south," she explained. "It's the lion by the steps. We walked south till we reached the wall at the end of the garden, and we stopped by the little pool and looked, just in case there was something."

"But there wasn't," Ashley interrupted.

"Except we found a lion's face on the wall, all covered with ivy and stuff."

"So we thought we'd come and ask you," Rachel ended, helplessly.

"Down by the pool wur you?" asked Digby. "Used to look proper pretty down there," he continued, talking to himself. "Mister Leo, 'e liked it. Said the sound of water soothed 'im. Get down there and fix it one o' these days."

"Digby..." Rachel was getting impatient, but Digby wouldn't be hurried.

"Never liked it meself," he murmured. "Like a drippin' tap. But 'e liked the stupid, dribblin' creature." His shoulders shook in silent laughter and he looked at the puzzled faces. "Seems you're on the roight track, don't it?" The children shrugged.

"Found the first namesake?" They nodded.

"Now you've got another!" he grinned. "Get down there 'n' read'n again. Do what it sez." he shoved the clue at Rachel, nodding to himself with satisfaction. "Mister Leo were a caution ... Stupid, dribblin' creature!"

Rachel looked at Ashley and rolled her eyes, then she gave Digby the list and the raspberry message. "We'll collect the barrow later, Digby," she said.

They walked down to the pool, reading and rereading the clue. When they got there, Ashley pulled back the plants and Rachel stood frowning at the lion's head.

"Right, I'm going to read it once more, really carefully. And if we don't get it this time, we'll give up and go and rob a bank!" she announced fiercely.

Come on, Uncle Leo! What kind of game were you playing? Does it really have to be this hard?

74

"OK, here goes!

"One namesake faces south,
  Where another empties his mouth.

"What's all this about emptying mouths?" Rachel groaned. "I'm confused!" Ashley clung to the ivy, concentrating hard. Then he laughed.

"Stupid, dribblin' creature!" he shouted.

"Wha...?"

"Look! *That's* what Digby meant. It's a *fountain!* The water came out of that pipe thingy in its mouth and fell into the pool underneath. We're on the right track!"

Rachel danced round the pool, flapping the piece of paper. "Ash, you're like Sherlock Holmes! Let go of that stuff and help me look for the next clue. It's got to be here somewhere!"

They searched all round the edge of the pool, pulling at paving stones, searching for marks that might be secret signs. But they found nothing. Rachel sat back on her heels and pushed up her fringe.

"This *is* the right place," she said firmly. "We just aren't thinking properly. Come on, Ash, you're the one with the turbo-powered brain!"

"OK then, we do exactly what it says," said Ashley. "We followed the first lion to where the next one empties his mouth, yeah? So, now we look in his mouth!"

"You look, you're taller," said Rachel. "I'll hold the plants out of the way."

Ashley stretched across the wall and felt inside the lion's mouth. "I can feel the pipe," he said. "It's a bit wobbly ... just need to *pull* ... ooo!" The pipe suddenly came out, he lost his grip on the wall and overbalanced. One moment he was spread across the wall like Spiderman, the next he was sitting up to his waist in murky water. Rachel gave a horrified gasp, then collapsed in laughter.

"Sorry!" she choked, leaning over and offering Ashley a hand. He ignored her and waded to the edge of the pool, trying to look dignified, with water dripping down his legs and strands of pond weed tangling his feet. He crawled out and stood in a growing puddle, trying to control his feelings.

If she wasn't a girl, I'd smash her face in! I'm supposed to be on holiday. I didn't need to help her do this, did I?

Yeah, but you want to help. This thing's got hold of you now and you want to be in on it!

He held out a dripping arm and dropped the pipe in Rachel's hand. "There you are. I hope it's worth getting nearly drowned for!" He squelched off, stiff-legged and stern, towards the house.

"I'm sorry I laughed." Rachel hurried after him. "Wait, we need to get the barrow from Digby!"

"Get it yourself!" Ashley growled.

Ashley was pulling on clean socks, when there was a tap on his bedroom door.

"It's me," said Rachel's voice. "Can I come in?"

"OK."

She was carrying a glass of orange juice and a plate of buns. "To say sorry," she explained, looking at the heap of wet clothes. "You really are great, Ash, helping me like this. I promise I'll never laugh at you again."

Ashley shrugged. "It wasn't my newest T-shirt."

Rachel handed him the drink and buns, then pulled the pipe from her pocket. "Shall we look at it now?"

Ashley nodded.

"It's blocked," she informed him after peering in at one end.

"Digby said something needed fixing," he reminded her.

"I don't ever remember the fountain," said Rachel, "so it must have been broken for ages."

"Blocked, not broken," Ashley corrected her. "Get something to poke in – see if you can shift whatever's in there."

Rachel found some scissors. "You want to do it?" she offered. Ashley shook his head.

No way! I've had enough danger for one day. Knowing my luck, it'd blow up in my face or drop on my foot and break a toe!

He finished one bun and took another.

"It's jammed solid," muttered Rachel as she pushed and poked at the end of the pipe. "There's a lot of dirt in here," she said as she carefully scraped it out. "It won't budge."

"Try scraping out the other end," Ashley suggested.

"There's something solid in the middle. Shall I push hard?"

She put the pipe, end down, on the floor, stuck the scissors into the other end and then pushed down with all her weight. "It ... won't ... move," she panted.

"Put some effort into it!" Ashley grinned.

"I *am!*" she puffed. "It just won't ... Aaagh!" She sprawled across the floor as the pipe skidded under the bed and whatever had blocked it rolled across the floor and bounced off the wall.

Ashley forgot he wasn't going to get involved, dropped his half-eaten bun and pounced. Rachel scrambled to her knees, rubbing her nose.

"It's a sort of metal bottle, I think," he said, rolling the little cylinder in the palm of his hand. "Look, it's got a screw-on lid at one end."

"It's an old medicine tube," said Rachel. "Mum's got some that she keeps buttons and needles in. She told me they used to sell things like cough sweets in these. Before plastic, you know?"

Ashley peered closely. "Oh yes. Look, you can still see a bit of the writing on the side. 'One to be sucked every two...' "

"It's one of Uncle Leo's cough sweet tubes!" Rachel interrupted. "Quick, open it!"

The lid was old and rusty, but at last Ashley managed to unscrew it. Then he handed it to Rachel. "Go on, you do it."

She shook it impatiently, but nothing came out.

"Calm down," said Ashley. "Don't be in such a rush. Feel inside with your finger."

She did and out came a thin roll of paper.

"Yes!" hissed Ashley fiercely. Rachel unrolled the paper and spread it on the floor. They both crouched over it.

"Huh! Another poem!" Ashley sat back.

"OK," laughed Rachel, "but it's another clue and that's what matters."

Ashley sighed. "Let's hear it then. I can hardly wait!"

"It's a bit smudged," said Rachel, screwing up her eyes.

"James Grieve, Arthur Turner, Lord Derby;
Long-standing, straight, no tangle.
Next 'here we go round';
Then deep in the right-angle."

"This isn't difficult; it's impossible!" said Ashley.

"No," Rachel replied thoughtfully, "I think the clues are easier for people who were close to Uncle Leo and know Yaffle House well."

"You may have a chance then," said Ashley, licking crumbs from his fingers. "And people like Digby, who worked for him. I wonder how long it is till lunch?"

Chapter 9

"Rachel, be a love and fetch down the pile of sheets on the landing," panted Tessa as she struggled past the living-room door with a load of towels. "We'll need to get a move on. There's folk arriving this afternoon and the beds aren't made up yet." She disappeared into the utility room, leaving a towel swinging gently on the door handle.

The weather was still hot. The sun shone brightly, and the air felt stale and heavy. All the doors and windows were open, but there was no breeze to bring relief. Ashley felt sticky and irritable.

"Do it later!" he muttered at Rachel. "We've got things to do." After finding the second clue, they both wanted to carry on searching without interruptions. But Rachel shook her head.

"No, I must do it. It's one of my holiday jobs."

Ashley scowled. "Why can't your precious guests make their own beds?" he asked. "They come and stay here and hardly pay a bean, and then they expect to be waited on. I think the whole thing's stupid!" Ashley still couldn't get used to the way Yaffle House worked.

Fancy doing all this work and being so nice to people and then not make any money out of them. No wonder they're broke!

"Maybe they would make their own beds if we

asked them to," Rachel said, "but some of them come here for a rest. We want them to be happy and not be rushing about doing jobs."

"Sounds stupid to me," Ashley replied.

"Do you have a problem with being nice to people?" demanded Rachel. "Is there something wrong with wanting to make people happy?"

"Huh!"

"What's got into you, Ash? You've been ratty since breakfast!"

"Nothing!" Ashley growled.

But it hadn't been nothing. He'd had a bad night. It had been hard to get to sleep and he seemed to toss about for hours. When he finally did fall asleep, he had that dream again. It was a bit different, but the place and the feelings were just the same. It was pitch dark, like before, and he was back in the closed-in place. He was frightened. And, just like the last dream, he knew he wasn't alone in the darkness; someone else was in there with him. This time there was a faint, whispery voice that he vaguely recognised, calling his name.

"Ash! Hey, Ash! Where are you, man?" The voice grew louder and clearer.

"Hey, Ash! Are you one of us? We need a decision, man. Know what I'm sayin'?"

"Jax!" breathed a frightened voice in his head. "It's Jax and the Spookz! They won't wait for ever. You need to decide!"

His fear grew. He desperately wanted to get away. The cardboard cut-outs he'd put in the dark cupboard when he first arrived were becoming real again, and now he was trapped inside, with them! More voices joined in as Ashley found himself groping along the same wall, hands shaking and breath coming in panicky gasps.

"We need to know ... need to be sure of you."

"Don't upset me, Ash. We don't want trouble, do we?"

"C'mon, Ash ... C'mon, Ash ... Ash ... Ash..."

His fingers found the door handle and he hung on tight. Then there was that knocking again. Someone was outside, wanting to come in.

"What'll I do?" he whispered into the darkness. "I've got to choose. If I want to get out of the dark and away from Jax and the Spookz, I've got to open the door."

He woke with a jump. It was light and there were birds singing. He could hear the regular squeak of Digby's wheelbarrow passing the house. His breathing became calmer and he turned on his side, gazing round the room. The quiet ordinariness of his surroundings made him feel better. Yesterday's clothes lay jumbled on the floor by his bed; the headphones from his Walkman dangled from a half-opened drawer. He lay still, breathing slowly as the fear drained away, leaving him relaxed but, if he was being honest, not completely peaceful. The darkness hadn't all gone. Some of it was still there and it seemed to have got inside him.

I need to decide about the Spookz ... soon.

"You could always come and help me," said Rachel persuasively. "Then we'd finish quicker and we could get on with searching."

"OK," said Ashley grudgingly. "Let's get it over with."

The washing machine was full and churning busily, so they dumped the sheets in a heap and went outside into the glaring sunshine. Heat bounced up from the ground and the light was dazzling.

"Phew!" gasped Ashley.

"Where to next?" asked Rachel as they crossed the courtyard.

"Nowhere near that pond!" said Ashley firmly. "I know it's hot, but I'm not swimming in that again!"

"Let's go up the hill into the wood," suggested Rachel. "It'll be cooler up there."

Despite the heat Rachel bounded off, and Ashley struggled to keep up with her. His T-shirt was sticking to him by the time they reached the top of the hill. Rachel was right though – it was cool up in the wood and his bad mood seemed to have gone.

"Sorry about earlier," he grunted.

"No problem!" said Rachel. "You worried about something?"

"Yeah, something at home," Ashley shrugged his shoulders. "It's a gang at school ... the Spookz. They want me to do something ... I can't decide. I've been having bad dreams. Can't stop thinking about it."

"Can I help?"

"No, I'll sort it out."

Ashley stared at the countryside below him. The green and yellow fields shimmered in the heat.

"Everything feels better in the light," he murmured, pushing the Spookz firmly back into the dark cupboard again.

"Wonder if it'll rain," said Rachel, staring out at the distant clouds.

Surrounded by tall beech trees, like silver pillars, they sat on an old tree trunk and studied the second clue. Sunlight filtered down through the leaves far above, making little puddles of brightness.

"Right," said Rachel, very business-like. "We need to think slowly and carefully."

"OK," Ashley agreed. "Who are these three men it talks about?"

"Old friends of Uncle Leo's?" suggested Rachel. "Dad might know."

"Or Digby? He's *very* old."

"All right, Sherlock. Let's go and find him!" Rachel was off down the hill again.

"I've only just recovered from climbing *up* here!" Ashley groaned. "If I have a heart attack, who'll help you then?" he shouted at the empty path.

"Ha-ha-ha-ha!" There was a flash of green as a woodpecker flew by. Ashley sighed and started to follow Rachel. He found her waiting impatiently in the kitchen garden.

"Digby!" she shouted, spinning in a circle and shading her eyes from the sun. "Oh, where *is* he when we need him!"

There was the familiar squeak of the wheelbarrow and Digby appeared through the gate. Rachel dashed the length of the garden, with Ashley not far behind.

"Digby!" she panted, collapsing against the barrow and pushing her hair off her damp forehead. "James Grieve, Arthur Turner and Lord Derby; were they friends of Uncle Leo's?"

Digby slowly put down the barrow and straightened up. He wiped his hands very deliberately and pushed his cap back to scratch his head.

"They wuz, in a way."

"Well, who were they?" Rachel demanded.

There was a long pause.

"Not *who*," chuckled Digby. "They be *whats!*"

Rachel and Ashley looked at each other helplessly.

"Them's Mister Leo's favourite apple trees," Digby explained, walking slowly to the back of the garden. "Good croppers, all of 'em."

"Long standing ... straight...," Rachel read as they looked at the line of old trees standing along one wall.

"But there are *four* apple trees," Ashley interrupted, pointing at the last one in the row.

"T'ain't no apple," Digby grunted as he plodded back to his wheelbarrow. "'Tis a *mulberry*, that'n."

"Yes!" laughed Rachel. "Here's James Grieve, Arthur Turner and Lord Whatsit, standing straight and tall. And then 'Here we go round the mulberry bush' in the corner. *Now* it's starting to make sense!"

Ashley sighed wearily. "My brain hurts! What about the right-angle bit? That sounds like maths to me."

They walked along the line of trees and around behind the mulberry which stood right in the corner of the garden, where the two high walls met. Ashley took the clue from Rachel and frowned. "'Deep in the right-angle'," he said, looking down at a large stone that was half buried in the soil. "I think we need a spade!"

Soon he was digging around the stone.

"Can you get the edge of the spade under it now?" Rachel asked as she pulled up the long grass around the stone. Ashley tried, and together they pushed on the handle and slowly levered up the stone. As it rolled aside, Rachel dived forward and began to dig furiously with a trowel they had found with the spade.

Ashley helped her and soon there was a large hole. "It did say *deep* in the right-angle," he panted. On they dug until Rachel could hardly reach the bottom of the hole, then...

"Ah!" grunted Ashley. The spade had scraped something hard.

"It's one of Uncle Leo's tobacco tins!" said Rachel excitedly as Ashley pulled out something flat and dirty. Quickly she rubbed off the dirt. It was old and rusty, but they exchanged triumphant smiles as she handed it back to him.

"Your turn," she said. "You found it, anyway."

But the lid was rusted on and wouldn't budge.

"Bash it with a stone!" suggested Rachel, growing impatient again.

"Might be something inside that'd break," Ashley warned. "We need something to push the lid off."

They fetched Patrick's toolbox and used a screwdriver to try and force off the lid.

"Nothing's happening," Rachel groaned. "What about this hammer?"

"No," said Ashley. "Let me try again."

"Come on, come *on!*" pleaded Rachel through gritted teeth.

"There!" panted Ashley as the lid jerked off.

Ashley took out a small piece of folded paper.

"Clue number three, Sherlock!" cried Rachel in delight. "What's it say?"

"Oh, you're going to enjoy this!" Ashley laughed, after he'd unfolded it.

"High time, short point at four.
Climb a lofty guardian;
What stops his roar?"

Rachel clutched her head and rolled her eyes. "*What*? Oh, Uncle Leo, we don't have much time, you know!"

Chapter 10

The fat pink face smiled, showing a lot of very white teeth. The pudgy right hand with the glinting signet ring was held out confidently.

"Hi, Miles Doubleby's the name. We've spoken on the phone a number of times. Nice to meet you at last, Mr and Mrs Butterworth."

Patrick and Tessa shook hands politely with their unwelcome visitor and then stood aside to let him come in. Ashley shuddered as a cold shadow seemed to fill the hallway.

"*So* good of you to let me call round. I promise not to keep you long. Oh, and this is Tamara; she'll be assisting me."

A thin woman in a black suit and spikey-heeled shoes stalked in after him. She had scarlet finger-nails that matched her lips, and she carried a brief-case and a clipboard.

Ashley and Rachel, peering through the crack in the almost shut living-room door, had a good view of what was happening in the hall.

"Look at him!" hissed Rachel. "He thinks he owns the place."

"Shh!" said Ashley sharply.

"Mr Doubleby," Patrick was saying, "we need to tell you right away that we have no plans for sell-ing this house." Patrick had been annoyed when he heard how Mr Doubleby had persuaded Tessa to let him to see Yaffle House. However, he'd agreed to the visit because "He'll only keep pestering if we don't and I'd like to speak to him face to face. Maybe he'll understand then!" Ashley and Rachel were relieved – their plans wouldn't be wasted. Patrick stood now, in the middle of the hall, politely determined. Mr Doubleby's polished smile wavered and he seemed to shrink a bit as Patrick confronted him.

Yeah, just look at the Boffin! He may look weedy, but he's not scared of Pig Face. I reckon he could handle anyone, even Jax!

Mr Doubleby quickly recovered himself. "I *quite* understand, Mr Butterworth. Of course, of *course*. But if, in the future, you might *happen* to ... er ... change your mind, I want you to be secure in the knowledge that you have a definite buyer who will give you a *generous* price for this ... ah ... *delightful* property."

Rachel was clutching her stomach and pretending to be sick as the oily voice went on and on. Ashley watched the visitors intently, his hands clenched.

"I hope they visit the rooms in the right order," he muttered.

"Don't worry," Rachel assured him, "Dad won't change his route. He said he'll only be showing him the rooms that haven't got guests in, and he gave me a list."

"Didn't he wonder why you wanted to know?"

"Don't worry, I didn't tell him we were planning to put a few surprises round the house," Rachel giggled. "I just said we wanted to make sure we didn't get in the way!"

The group set off on a tour of the house. As they disappeared into the guests' lounge Ashley and Rachel crept from their hiding place, scuttled across the hall and flattened themselves against the wall outside, peering cautiously through the crack at the hinge-side of the door. Patrick and Tessa were standing in the middle of the large sunny room while Mr Doubleby and Tamara roamed around, making loud comments and taking notes.

"*Lovely* bit of moulding on the ceiling ... Window frames need attention ... Looks like damp in the corner there ... That fireplace is superb ... looks original ... Is it, Mr Butterworth?" Patrick muttered something. Then there was a shriek from Tamara.

"Eek! In the hearth! There's something dead! Oh, how *revolting!*"

There were gasps and anxious murmurings.

"Only a few twigs and feathers. Nothing to be scared of ... I think," Mr Doubleby's voice drawled.

"Probably just a bird's nest," suggested Tessa helpfully.

"It's about time the chimneys were swept. We often get rooks building nests in them," Patrick added.

Rachel and Ashley exchanged grins of delight, then dived across the hall to stand innocently by the office door as Patrick led the visitors across to the dining room.

"Quick!" hissed Rachel and they tore down the passage to collect a plastic box with holes in the lid which they carried carefully into the utility room. By the time the tour party reached the kitchen area at the back of the house, Rachel and Ashley were hiding beside the water butt in the yard, close to the open back door. They could hear Mr Doubleby's voice in the kitchen and then the sound of footsteps coming down the passage.

"Ah, the *laundry*, I presume?" said Mr Doubleby. "A trifle cramped, isn't it? Just as well you run such a *small* business here."

"We manage," came Tessa's terse reply.

"Drains! When were the drains last checked? This plumbing is rather antiquated, and you're so near the river there could well be..."

There was another shriek – louder this time.

"In the sink! Something moved!"

"Dear me," Patrick's calm voice wafted through the open door. "We seem to have a plague of frogs."

There was a scuffling sound and the elegant Tamara burst out into the yard, breathing heavily and clutching her clipboard with white-knuckled fingers. Mr Doubleby followed her, not looking quite so smooth now.

"I am *not* going back in there!" Tamara hissed at him through gritted teeth. "This place is positively *medieval!*"

"Stop fussing and let's get on," he snapped. "We've got in here at last. We need to make the most of the opportunity." The smile came back into his voice as Tessa appeared in the doorway.

"Is everything all right?" she asked. Ashley could hear a wobble of laughter in her voice. "I'm *so* sorry about the frogs. I can't think how they got in there, but then it is a bit damp in this corner of the house."

"Shall we take a look upstairs now?" suggested Mr Doubleby smoothly.

"Very well," agreed Patrick. "Just so long as you understand that we can only show you rooms that are unoccupied."

"That's perfectly all right, Mr Butterworth. Do lead on!"

"Right!" Rachel sprang from behind the water butt, dragging Ashley behind her. "They'll go up the main stairs, so we'll be quicker going up the back way."

A small, dark shape with dirty paws and muddy nose appeared at their feet. Rachel paused.

"Oh Moley, you've been digging again, haven't you?"

"He'd better not come," said Ashley doubtfully.

"I'll shut him in the living room," said Rachel, grabbing him by the collar.

A few moments later Ashley was following Rachel up the back stairs. At the door marked Private that led out on to the main landing they stopped and listened cautiously.

"Such a wonderful atmosphere ... Full of old-world charm ... Particularly like that chandelier in the stairwell..."

"Huh, Pig Face is still laying on the charm," muttered Ashley.

"Sick-making," Rachel agreed. "I wonder how charming he'll find the Blue Room?" She chuckled wickedly. Ashley felt something cold on his leg.

"Ray!" he hissed. "The Mole's got out!"

Rachel grabbed him and shrugged cheerfully at Ashley.

Easing the door open, they strained to hear what was happening in the bedroom across the landing. It wasn't long before Tamara staggered out. She was breathing deeply and fanning herself with her clipboard.

"It *is* rather a strong smell," came Tessa's voice. "I can only think it must be the drains."

"Or a dose of Harpole's best, double-strength manure," murmured Rachel as she struggled to hold on to the Mole.

Tamara rolled her eyes and glared at Mr Doubleby as he joined her on the landing.

"Miles, this is ridiculous," she protested in a fierce whisper. Mr Doubleby ignored her, swept past and into the bedroom next door. Tamara sighed and started to follow him, when she realised she was being glared at by a small black dog. The Mole had finally managed to escape and now he was sitting in the middle of the landing, just out of Rachel's reach, with a fierce frown on his face. Tamara shuddered.

"Revolting creature!" she muttered to herself.

A hint of a growl rumbled in the back of the Mole's throat as Tamara hurried after Mr Doubleby.

"Rachel!" Patrick's voice was stern. "I know you're lurking here somewhere. Will you please remove that animal *at once!*" Rachel slid swiftly through the door, flashed an apologetic smile at her father and, tucking the Mole under her arm, dived back into the Annexe.

"Oh brilliant!" She was ecstatic. "Boxes of manure under the beds! Ash, you're a genius! Quick, it's the cellar next. Is everything ready?"

Ashley nodded and reached into his pocket, bringing out a light-bulb and a screwdriver.

Hurtling back down the stairs and along the

passage to the study, almost opposite the cellar door, they managed to hide behind the door just as Patrick and the others arrived from the front of the house.

"I *particularly* want to look at the cellar," Mr Doubleby was saying. "With some imagination a person could do *such* clever things ... a sauna ... gymnasium...!"

Ashley and Rachel could see Patrick fumbling in his pocket for the cellar key, Tessa looking fed up, and the back of Mr Doubleby's chubby pink neck bulging slightly over his smart white collar. The door was unlocked and opened, then there was a click.

"Sorry, the bulb seems to have blown," Patrick said mildly.

"Not to worry, Mr Butterworth. We came prepared. Torch please, Tamara!"

Tamara balanced on one leg as she rummaged through her briefcase for a torch.

"Watch the steps, they're rather steep," Patrick warned as four pairs of feet clumped down the wooden stairs. Soon the voices faded.

"Right, here goes!" said Ashley. They crept across the passage, and Rachel cautiously closed the cellar door while Ashley took the screwdriver from his pocket.

"Quick!" she hissed. "They may not stay down long."

"I'm going as fast as I can," Ashley muttered, furiously turning the screwdriver. "I'm glad we loosened the screws a bit before. There! One pull and the whole handle'll drop off!"

Soon they heard approaching footsteps. The door

handle waggled and then dropped with a satisfying clunk to the floor. Muffled voices sounded surprised and annoyed.

"Sorry ... handle was rather old..."

"Got another appointment in half an hour ... most inconvenient..."

"Battery's going flat ... trapped here for ever!"

Someone started banging on the door and shouting.

"I'll go and tell Mrs Latchett there's nothing to worry about," said Rachel. "We don't want her letting them out too soon!" She was back again quickly. "She can't hear – she's hanging out washing."

More banging and shouting. Rachel looked at Ashley, and he looked at his watch and shook his head.

"Just a bit longer. Let them get really worked up."

At last it was time. Ashley picked up the door handle and shoved it through the hole. There was some rattling and thumping and the door flew open. Mr Doubleby was first out, brushing cobwebs from his suit and smoothing back his hair. Tamara followed, her scarlet lips pressed into an angry slit. Patrick and Tessa came last, looking calm but rather puzzled.

"We really must dash," gasped Mr Doubleby. "Thank you for showing us round your, er, charming house." He hurried to the front door, with Tamara tottering after him. On the front step he turned.

"We'll be in touch, Mr Butterworth!"

"Eeeek!" Tamara stood clutching her briefcase and clipboard to her chest and pointing with a shaking finger. There, sitting by the passenger door of Mr Doubleby's car, was the Mole. From his mouth dangled a very dead rat. He laid it down and bared his teeth at Tamara.

"It's snarling at me!" she shuddered.

"*Rachel!*" Patrick hardly ever raised his voice, but now he did. Rachel, dog and dead rat quickly disappeared. Mr Doubleby left the drive in a shower of gravel, his mobile phone clamped to his ear. In the silence that followed, Ashley felt the warm sun again. The shadow had gone.

"Phew!" Tessa sat down on the top step. Patrick joined her and they leaned on each other, looking tired. Ashley waited awkwardly nearby.

Will they guess it was us who put all those things in the rooms?

"Come and join us, Ashley," said Tessa.

"Can we come back now?" Rachel appeared, with the Mole. There was no sign of the dead rat.

"We asked you to keep Moley out of the way," Patrick said sternly. "He really upset Tamara."

"Well, *she* upset *him!*" Rachel retorted. "I think he was just getting his own back!"

She joined the other three on the doorstep, and Tessa gave her a hug.

"Poor Moley, she was very rude to you," she said, tickling the dog's ears.

"And he wasn't snarling at her," Rachel continued indignantly. "He was *smiling!*"

Patrick looked annoyed. "I'd like to know what you two have been up to this morning!" he said quietly.

Chapter 11

"Well, if we've put Pig Face off trying to buy the house, it hasn't been a total waste of time, has it?" sighed Rachel gloomily. She and Ashley were sitting in a shady corner of the stable yard, while the sun beat down. Even in the shade the heat was intense, and it was hard to concentrate.

"What'll we do this afternoon?" Ashley yawned, poking the cobblestones with a stick.

"We ought to keep on looking," said Rachel, not very enthusiastically.

"After what Patrick said?" Ashley was thinking about what had happened after Mr Doubleby's visit that morning.

"Mr Doubleby and Tamara were visitors," Patrick had said sternly. "The way they were treated was inexcusable."

"But, Dad, we didn't *invite* them!" Rachel protested. "They weren't proper visitors."

"Nevertheless, they came into our home and were badly treated," Patrick continued.

"Pat, Pig Fa ... Mr Doubleby *is* awful," said Tessa. "But I suppose the poor man can't help the way he is," she added.

Ashley was amazed.

There they go again, being nice to people! He

doesn't care about our feelings, so why bother about his?

"But we had to *do* something!" Rachel explained.

Patrick sighed. "I know it's hard when things seem to be going against us, but we need to trust God to help us."

"We understand what you were trying to do," said Tessa, and she smiled at Rachel and Ashley. "It was really clever and ... and very funny," she stopped and chuckled. "But no more frogs or awful smells, OK? Oh, and no more dead rats either, Moley – do you hear?"

"If Tessa and Patrick won't let us help, we'd better stop looking for the loot then," said Ashley.

Rachel shook her head. "We *must* carry on!" she insisted. "They won't mind if we just look, as long as we don't do anything else to Mr Doubleby."

"I can think of a few more things I'd like to do to him!" growled Ashley, then he shivered.

"What's the matter?" Rachel asked.

"It makes everything feel dark, just thinking about him," said Ashley. "Like the dream I keep having ... I'm shut in this dark place with some people I don't really like. They're dark ... everything they do and say is dark."

"The Spookz?" asked Rachel.

Ashley nodded. "Sometimes I think I'd really like to be in the Spookz, and then I think I don't want to be like them because of some of the things they do," he explained, feeling a bit silly. "I'm scared they'll beat me up if I don't join them, and I'm scared that I'm like them already because I sometimes do things that are wrong."

"Want some help?" asked Rachel.

"I keep thinking it'd be OK if I could get rid of the dark, but I just can't make it go," said Ashley.

" 'The light shines in the darkness and the darkness has never put it out'," said Rachel quietly.

"Uh?"

"It says that in the Bible – about Jesus," Rachel explained. "Dad says Jesus is like a light. God sends him to shine his love into us and help us get rid of the dark things inside us."

"Light's sort of stronger than the dark," Ashley agreed. "You can't have light and dark both in the same place, can you?"

"Mm, so if you let Jesus bring the light inside you the darkness just ... has to go!"

"How does he get in?" Ashley really wanted to know.

"He waits quietly till people ask him. He doesn't barge in."

"Like Pig Face!"

"He only comes in if we want him to take the dark away."

Light that comes in and keeps the dark away? I like that! Ray and her family seem to be full of light. They're not always wanting things and fighting. Light seems to shine out of them, too. I'd like to be like them. Jax and the Spookz make me feel dark. I don't think I want to be like them. But I've got to choose. Do I join the Spookz or do I let Jesus bring the light in?

Rachel was looking at him, waiting. "Need to work out this clue," he grunted. Rachel spread the third clue on the cobbles between them and they studied it wearily. They both sighed. The stable yard shimmered in the afternoon heat, and Ashley squinted through the sunshine at the building opposite. He ran his hands though his damp hair and tried desperately to think.

It's up to us now. What can we do? It's like we're fighting something that's bigger and stronger than us. We're just too small to win...

" 'High time'," Ashley grunted. "OK, let's start looking at clocks then!"

Rachel nodded.

"And he'd have to be sure that it wasn't a clock that might be moved, otherwise that'd spoil his clue," Ashley added.

Rachel looked worried. "How could Uncle Leo be sure that someone wouldn't move the clock in his clue?"

Ashley looked smug. "I think I know," he said, staring across the yard at the coach house opposite. Rachel followed his gaze and saw the stable clock in its little tower, high up on the roof.

"Ohh!" she whispered quietly. "I'd forgotten it was there. I don't remember hearing the bell ring for ages."

"Well it's stayed at five to six ever since we got here," Ashley pointed out. "It's probably broken, like the fountain."

"Will that matter, d'you think?" Rachel wondered.

"Hang on," interrupted Ashley. "I'm just thinking about the second bit of the clue."

Rachel watched him expectantly, hands clenched between her knees.

" 'Short point at four'," Ashley continued. "What do you point with?"

"A finger?" Rachel suggested.

"And where are your fingers?"

"On your ... *hands!*" she shouted as she realised what he was suggesting. "So, if it was four o'clock" – she scrambled up and leapt into the sunlight, staring up at the clock – "the short hand would be pointing at four." She looked back at Ashley and he nodded.

"It's Uncle Leo's style all right," he agreed.

"So, it's something to do with a number four then?" Rachel suggested.

"Or what if it's like the first clue?" replied Ashley. "You know, where we had to walk in the direction that the lion was facing."

Rachel was excited. "Let's try it!"

"Right," said Ashley. "We need to think of a line that starts in the centre of the clock and comes out through the four..." He tried to draw the line in the air.

Rachel nodded again, looking up at his pointing finger, then turning slowly and following an imaginary line down to the right.

"Of *course!*" she laughed. "The 'lofty guardian'!"

Ashley turned towards the stone lion that stood on the top of the arched gateway, and he groaned.

Oh no! No way is she getting me up there! A dirty pond is one thing; breaking my neck is something else! It's her house, it's her uncle and this is definitely her problem!

"Ash, you are *brill*-iant!" Rachel gasped. "How do you do it?"

Ashley stepped back quickly, just in case she decided to hug him. "Need a ladder," he said.

They found one in the coach house, which they heaved across the yard to the arch. They were both dripping with sweat by this time.

"Well?" puffed Rachel, looking up at the lion and then back at Ashley. "I suppose it's my turn to do something. Will you hold the ladder please?"

Ashley was relieved that he didn't need to admit that he couldn't stand heights. He watched with admiration as Rachel hauled herself up until she was sitting astride the wall.

"That was easy enough," she panted. "Now for the tricky bit!" Slowly she began to work her way along the wall and up onto the arch, arms and legs gripping like a monkey

"Careful, Ray," Ashley called. "Don't hurry." He dug his clenched fists deep into his pockets. He could hardly bear to look. "Don't look down!" he pleaded quietly.

How can she do it? I bet she wouldn't be scared of Jax's Test. The Spookz! Why do they keep coming into my mind? I don't want to think about them!

"Done it!" Rachel had reached the lion and was hanging on to its front paws. "Now what?" she called down.

Ashley looked at the clue. " 'What stops his roar?' L ... Look inside his mouth," he called up.

He clamped both hands over his mouth. His eyes were riveted on Rachel's figure high above his head.

She reached up and felt inside the lion's open mouth, then she was waving something in her hand.

"What is it?"

"A parcel. Mind, I'll throw it down!"

Ashley jumped backwards as the small parcel thudded onto the cobbles beside him. "Hey!" he shouted, starting to unwrap it. "Look!"

But Rachel wasn't looking; she was clinging to the archway with her face pressed against the bricks.

"Ray!" yelled Ashley. "Come down!"

"Can't!" came the muffled reply.

"What's the matter?"

"I ... I can't do it!"

"You've got to!"

She shook her head.

Ashley stared around in panic and then he swallowed and called up to her. "It's OK, I'm coming up!"

What am I saying? I get dizzy sleeping on a top bunk! I don't climb anything, especially not wonky ladders and high brick walls!

Looking straight ahead, he climbed up the ladder. "I'm coming!" he called, hoping he sounded reassuring. "Don't look down!" he muttered to himself as he scrambled onto the wall and began to edge along. The arch seemed far higher now, and he had to look up to see the soles of Rachel's trainers above him.

"I'm behind you," he called. "I'm going to get hold of your right foot and move it back a little bit. Are you ready? It'll be OK. All you have to do is move one bit of you at a time. There's no hurry."

Reaching up, he gripped her ankle. He felt her go tense, but she moved it a tiny bit.

"That's great! Now a bit more. Ready?"

This time she moved further and then shuffled her body backwards a little. Ashley moved back too, and so it went on.

"Nearly there," panted Ashley as he felt the ladder

against his leg. For a second he saw the ground far below. His stomach lurched as he fought the panic. Then gritting his teeth and squeezing his eyes tight shut, he swung over the wall and felt with his feet for the rungs of the ladder. He scrambled down as fast as his shaking legs would let him, and stood back as Rachel followed. As her feet touched the ground, she staggered and sat down heavily.

"You OK?" asked Ashley in a shaky voice. Rachel nodded. Her face was deathly pale.

"Thanks," she said faintly. "That was awful. It was like something was ... *leaning* on me, stopping me moving. I couldn't see properly ... I was inside a dark cloud." She looked around with relief at the dazzling sunshine. "If you hadn't come, I'd still be stuck up there."

Ashley shrugged. "If I hadn't got the idea, you wouldn't have gone up there in the first place," he reminded her.

"I found something, though," said Rachel, starting to look cheerful again. "Where is it?"

Ashley felt in his pocket and then held out the little parcel. Rachel carefully peeled the paper back and pulled out a large key.

"It's got something wrapped round it," Ashley pointed out.

Rachel unwound the thin strip of paper and held it out for Ashley to see as she read what was written there.

"Across ... above ... but near at hand;
Descend by three;
In cold and dark it waits;
Then search humbly."

"Good ol' Uncle Leo," Ashley groaned. "This is the worst yet!"

"But we've got a key now!" Rachel reminded him. "That *must* mean we're near the loot at last!"

Chapter 12

The phone rang during breakfast the next day. Patrick returned from answering it in the office and sat down quietly, picking up his half-eaten toast.

"Who was it?" asked Tessa.

"Someone wanting to book for next month."

"What did you say?"

"Just that we'd have to call them back in a week's time."

Rachel and Ashley stopped eating and exchanged glances.

"Dad, why aren't you taking bookings?" asked Rachel.

Slowly Patrick finished chewing. "We can't take bookings when we aren't sure what will happen next month," he said wearily.

"We still haven't done the work on the kitchen," Tessa explained.

"You mean we're going to close?" Rachel cut in sternly.

"I sincerely hope we don't have to," her father replied, "but the deadline is getting closer. We shall have to decide by the end of the week."

Tessa looked down at her plate and bit her lip. Patrick calmly drained his cup and pushed back his chair. "Excuse me, I need to go and talk to somebody."

After he had gone, Rachel exploded. "How can Dad be so calm?" she fumed. "Doesn't he care?"

"Of *course* he cares!" Tessa snapped back. Her face was flushed. "We're both worried sick, but yelling the place down doesn't help!"

Rachel flung herself on the floor, grabbed the Mole and sat rocking to and fro. Ashley watched helplessly.

So everything we've done is useless? If Yaffle House has to be sold, old Doubleby will have won. We need more time! If only daft ol' Uncle Leo hadn't hidden his loot so well!

The Mole was tired of being hugged. He licked Rachel's face and then struggled free. Rachel got up and put her arm round her mother's shoulders.

"Sorry," she said. "Ash and I are helping too," she added. Ashley nodded.

Tessa smiled. "I know you are, and don't worry – God's in charge and there's still time for things to work out." She glanced at her watch. "Heavens, look at the time!" She hauled herself off her chair. "Oof, it's hard to get going in this heat. The weather forecast says it's going to be hotter than ever today."

Rachel collected Mrs Latchett's list and they went to find Digby. The air felt hot and heavy as they plodded along the path with the Mole panting loudly behind them.

"We've *got* to find where the key fits soon," said Rachel. "It's getting urgent now!"

"I can't cope with 'urgent' in this heat," Ashley grumbled cheerfully. Despite everything, he was surprised how optimistic he felt. "We've worked out all the other clues," he reminded her. "I think we're *nearly* there!"

"Oh, I hope so," Rachel sighed. "I want Mum and Dad to be happy again."

"Who was Patrick going to talk to just now?" asked Ashley.

"God, probably," replied Rachel.

"What, praying an' that?"

"Yes. Dad says God's always there, listening and wanting to help. Only, I sometimes forget and start worrying. I expect that's why Dad doesn't get so worked up. He remembers God's on our side!"

"It's *got* to be a door," Rachel decided. "The key's too big to fit anything else."

"Why can't it be a treasure chest?" demanded Ashley. It was the afternoon and they were sitting in his room, studying the fourth clue.

"I told you before, that'd be too obvious," Rachel replied patiently.

"OK, well, it's across something and above us but near," said Ashley.

"Somewhere cold and dark, too," Rachel added.

"The cellar?" suggested Ashley.

"That's near but *below*," Rachel pointed out.

"A room upstairs, then?"

"Nah, they're not cold or dark!"

They were quiet for a while, thinking.

"Uncle Leo never seems to do things we expect. Maybe we shouldn't be looking in the house at all, just *near* it," said Ashley.

Rachel became alert. " 'Above'. Up a tree maybe? Or ... *up the hill!*"

"Worth a try," Ashley agreed.

They went slowly downstairs. As they passed the kitchen, they saw Mrs Latchett working, grim and silent, at the table. Ashley frowned.

This is really getting to everybody. There's a strange feeling in the air and I don't think it's just because of the weather.

In the yard they met Tessa looking worried. "If only it would *rain!*" she sighed, putting on a weak smile. "I feel as though my head's going to explode!" Rachel and Ashley crossed the river and climbed slowly up through the woods to the top of the hill.

"Hey, look at those clouds!" exclaimed Ashley as they stood at the gap in the trees on top of the hill. Huge mounds of white and dark grey were heaped up, filling the sky. The countryside below had changed colours in the strange light from the hidden sun.

"There's rain coming," said Rachel. "Feel the breeze?"

"Phew, about time too!"

"Well, we're 'above', but there's nothing here to fit a key into," Rachel looked around. They walked about, half-heartedly.

" 'Cold and dark'," quoted Ashley. "Bet it's cold up here in the winter."

"It is, but so's everywhere. It's got to mean more than that," replied Rachel.

There was a distant rumble.

"Thunder!" said Rachel, stopping abruptly. "We need to get back. Moley doesn't like thunder."

"What about the key?" Ashley protested, but Rachel didn't hear. He sighed and started back down the hill after her. Thunder rumbled again, nearer now. As they trudged down the last slope, with the river and house in sight, something between the trees caught his eye. He stopped and pointed.

109

"Ray!"

Rachel froze in mid-stride and followed Ashley's finger. Then she gave a wild yell and bounded off through the woods towards the strange little building below.

"The ice house!"

Ashley stumbled after her, branches whipping across his face, brambles snagging his legs, but excitement driving him on.

"We crossed the river to get here ... we're near the house *and* above it ... and this must have been a cold place when it was being used!" he panted as he joined Rachel. She wasn't listening, though.

"Help me pull this off!" she panted as she began ripping strands of ivy off the door. The sky grew dark, but they didn't notice. Soon the door was uncovered and she pushed the key into the lock.

"It fits!" She turned to Ashley, her eyes round with excitement.

"See if it'll turn," said Ashley tensely as thunder growled, nearer still.

Rachel's hands were shaking as the key clicked round loudly in the lock.

"Yes, oh yes, oh *yes!*" shouted Ashley, punching his fist into the air.

They pushed, but the door wouldn't open.

"Come *on!*" Ashley grunted, leaning hard with his shoulder.

"It's coming!" panted Rachel. The hinges creaked slightly as the door opened a crack, before sticking again.

"Nyaagh!" growled Ashley, kicking the door.

"Maybe the hinges need oiling?" suggested Rachel. "Let's get..."

"*Kerrr*-ASH!"

Both children jumped as a blinding flash of lightning and a deafening thunder-clap crackled out of the trees just above them. For a split second there was a stunned silence and then the rain came. Not just a few polite drops, warning that a proper shower was following, but a sudden Niagara Falls of a downpour that soaked them to the skin in seconds. The sky had grown dark and the wind gusted so that the trees began to lash and sway. The wood was no longer a friendly place to be. It was full of dark shapes flickering around tree trunks and leafy arms thrashing about. Angry voices seemed to growl and shriek.

"Moley!" yelled Rachel, stuffing the key back into her pocket and turning towards the house.

"Forget Moley, what about the door?" Ashley yelled. Another thunder crash sent him bolting after her, with rain streaming down his face and half-blinding him. "Wait for me!"

The storm lasted till evening, and, even though the wind blew less wildly and the thunder slowly faded away, the rain went on falling. Rachel and Ashley stood at the living-room windows, watching the garden through the streaming glass.

"As soon as it stop, we'll get the oil and go back out," said Rachel as she cuddled the Mole.

"Yeah," Ashley nodded, but without much enthusiasm. The storm had frightened him more than he wanted to admit. Fortunately, Tessa decided for them.

"Promise me you won't go out again this evening," she said. "There's still a bit of thunder about and Digby's just come by to say that the wind's brought a few trees down."

"But..." Rachel began.

"No, Rachel. It's not safe out there. What would Ashley's parents say if a tree fell on him!"

So they spent the evening watching TV and playing Scrabble, though neither of them was really concentrating.

"First thing tomorrow, OK?" whispered Rachel as they climbed the stairs to their rooms that night. Ashley nodded and yawned. It was cooler now and both of them fell asleep immediately.

Chapter 13

Ashley knew he was dreaming straight away. The darkness, the feelings, the whispering voices were all familiar this time.

"It's Decision Time, Ash," whispered the menacing voice, rumbling like distant thunder.

Ashley found himself edging along the wall, feeling the door under his back and fingers

"I'm gettin' impatient, man. Know what I'm sayin'? I want your decision *now!*"

They were getting closer than ever. Fear gripped him as the darkness seemed to grow darker than ever.

"Help me, somebody!" he gasped.

Then the knocking began again, steady and persistent.

"You're makin' me very angry, Ash," rasped the voice in the stifling darkness.

"The light!" shouted Ashley, suddenly remembering. He turned and flung himself against the door. He could feel the roughness of the wood against his cheek as he fumbled for the handle. "Jesus! I need your light, *quick!*" Ashley turned the handle, wrenching the door open.

"Time's up, man. I'm comin' to get..."

Ashley knew that Jesus had heard him. The light flooded in!

"Ready?" Rachel's head appeared round Ashley's bedroom door just after half past five the following morning. Ashley was up and dressed, standing looking out of the window. A watery sun was struggling through the final shreds of clouds. The fear and darkness had gone. He felt different now. He'd decided.

"It's a real mess out there," Rachel said, staring down at the twigs and broken branches scattered over the grass.

"It was the worst storm I've ever seen," said Ashley, "but it's all right now ... Everything's OK now."

Rachel looked puzzled. "What do you mean? We haven't found the treasure yet."

"Remember you were talking about Jesus bringing the light?" he said. "Well, it's starting to make sense." He tried to explain. "When I came here I could see your family were a bit ... different. Not weird or anything!" he added quickly. "Just, well, you think about things differently. It seems to be very important to do things the way you think God wants. You're happy without always buying new things, and ... you don't seem worried that you might lose the house."

"Some of us are, a *bit!*" Rachel said.

"OK, just a bit, but you don't get angry and start blaming other people."

Rachel listened quietly.

"So with you all talking about God and then finding out about the light, I wanted to be like you. I thought it might help me know what to do about the Spookz."

"You mean the dreams and having to decide?" asked Rachel.

"Yes. I think it'll be OK now."

"Oh?"

"Yes, last night I asked Jesus to bring the light in," Ashley replied quietly.

Rachel beamed.

"The dark's gone and I know what to do now. I don't need the Spookz. I don't want to do things that make me feel bad and dark. They can't *make* me be like them!"

Rachel nodded. "Jesus and the light will help you keep the darkness away. He'll be with you, showing you the right thing to do, all the time, everywhere – he's promised!"

"All the time, everywhere. He's promised," said Ashley firmly. They were both quiet for a moment and then Ashley looked at his watch.

"Come on, we mustn't waste time," he said.

"And we *must* be quiet," Rachel added. "We don't want to wake everyone else."

They crept down the creaky stairs and tip-toed to the back door.

"Shhh!" hissed Rachel as Ashley pulled back the top bolt with a bit of a clunk. Once outside, they hurried through the garden to the bridge.

"That was some storm!" panted Rachel as they jumped over fallen branches. "Hey, where's the path?"

Just beyond the bridge was a tangle of branches and tree trunks where the path up the hill had been.

"Why do trees look bigger when they're lying down?" wondered Ashley as he stared at the silver pillars tumbled this way and that.

"How are we going to get to the ice house?" said Rachel, being practical.

Ashley shivered suddenly. "Something's trying to stop us," he muttered, half to himself.

Rachel looked back at him. "We're going to get through, Ash," she said firmly.

It was a long, hard struggle, and by the time they reached the ice house they were scratched and dirty.

"Oh no!" wailed Rachel. Lying where the ice house had stood was a huge tree trunk.

"How'll we get through that lot?" gasped Ashley, staring at the bits of wall and splintered wood where the ice house had been.

"We aren't going to let this stop us," muttered Rachel fiercely, and she began to squirm under the tree trunk.

"Careful!" warned Ashley.

"It's OK, there's a space on the other side!" came Rachel's muffled voice. Ashley looked doubtfully at the little gap, then started after her.

"I think I've crushed all my ribs!" he complained as he dragged himself up on the far side of the tree trunk, but Rachel wasn't listening.

"Look, you can see where the door was," she said.

Ashley laughed. "Won't be needing the key now, will we?"

Together they knelt among the broken branches and splintered planks, and peered down into a dark hole.

"Got the torch?" asked Rachel in a shaky voice.

"Uh-huh."

"Who's going first this time?"

"Me, I'm bigger," Ashley answered, trying to sound brave.

He switched on the torch and shone the beam down into the hole. "Here goes!" He climbed over the remains of the door, ducked under a large branch and disappeared from sight.

"Ash?" called Rachel anxiously.

"It goes down!" Ashley shouted back. "There're steps!"

"How many?" Rachel hardly dared ask.

"Guess!"

"What? *Three*? Oh, wait for me!" And she scrambled through to join him. There was just room to stand together at the bottom of the three stone steps. The broken roof and walls were like a gloomy cave, with leaves and branches poking through.

"I don't think it's very safe," Ashley warned as a chunk of brick tumbled down beside him.

" 'Search humbly'," muttered Rachel. "How do you do *that*?"

"No idea," Ashley replied, kneeling down to examine the steps.

"Like that!" Rachel exclaimed. "Kneeling means you're being humble!" She grabbed his hand and shone the torch on to the floor just where it joined the bottom step. "Look!" Very faintly they could see where the initials L.B. had been scratched, years before, while the cement was still soft.

"Leo Butterworth! This is the place," whispered Rachel.

"We'll need tools to move that step," Ashley pointed out. "And we need to be quick!" More pieces of brick clattered down as a large branch above them shifted.

"Reckon you'll be needin' this!"

The voice came from above them and they both jumped with fright. Squinting up out of the hole they saw a familiar head and shoulders peering down, the light shining pink through his protruding ears.

"*Digby!*" gasped Rachel. "What're *you* doing here?"

"Seein' to things," he replied, slowly raising the bulging toolbag he carried.

Rachel and Ashley scrambled up to the door of the ruin and allowed Digby to squeeze past. He produced a chisel and a hammer, and soon there were bits of cement flying. Then out came a crowbar and he began to lever up the stone that formed the top of the step.

"How did you know?" gasped Rachel.

"Remembered, sudden like," Digby grunted as he heaved at the step.

Ashley looked at him, suspicious. "How come you only just remembered?"

Digby looked straight back, his blue eyes bright and innocent. "Must've been the roight time."

"It's moving!" Rachel interrupted. With a final heave, the stone step slid onto the floor with a dull klonk and all three leaned forward to look.

"Phew!" whistled Ashley.

"There's your treasure chest, Ash!" laughed Rachel in a quavering voice.

Set into a hollowed-out space under where the stone step had rested was a small black metal box.

"Quick!" shrieked Rachel as the walls around them began to crumble. Digby grabbed the box and handed it up to her.

"Time to go," he growled.

A cloud covered the sun, plunging everything into sudden gloom. Ashley shivered again. "You're too late! You can't stop us now!" he whispered as he stared out into the wood. The shadows disappeared, and the sun glowed warm and reassuring.

"The light shines in the darkness and the darkness has never put it out."

"Ashley, wake up and help Digby!" Rachel ordered briskly, and between them they helped Digby haul himself out. With a final rumble, the hole disappeared and the tree trunk settled down firmly on top of it.

"Just in time!" panted Rachel.

The three of them struggled back through the wood and down on to the bridge. The sun shone, sparkling the water that chattered beneath them. Rachel laid the box down on the bridge, and she and Ashley crouched over it.

"Oh, I can't do it!" said Rachel with her hand poised over the lid. "What if it's empty?"

"Open it, for goodness sake. I'm getting hungry!" Ashley groaned.

Rachel gripped the lid and pulled it open.

"Oh!" she said, looking uncertainly at a cloth bundle.

"Wow!" gasped Ashley as she unwrapped it.

"Digby, *look!*" Rachel's voice was small and trembled as she held up a heavy gold necklace. The sun glinted off large green stones surrounded by many smaller white ones. "There's a bracelet, too ... and ... and lots of other things. It really is treasure!"

"Emeralds?" asked Ashley, looking up at Digby.

"Ar, an' pearls," he replied, nodding happily.

119

"They're *beautiful!*" whispered Rachel.

"Don't need to rob a bank now!" said Ashley.

Rachel had been staring dreamily at the sparkling heap in her hands, but suddenly she snapped back into action.

"Quick! We've got to show Mum and Dad!" She scrambled to her feet, carefully scooping the jewels into the rolled-up front of her sweater. Then clutching the bundle tightly to her chest, she set off for the house. But she was back again almost at once.

"Oh, *Digby!*" she gasped, trying to hug him with one arm. Ashley stood back quickly. He still didn't fancy being hugged!

Then she was away again, galloping across the grass towards the house. Ashley and Digby heard her voice floating back to them.

"Thank you, thank you, *thank you*, God! Mum! Daaaad!"

"Tearin' rush, that'n," observed Digby as she disappeared into the house.

"It's going to be OK now, isn't it?" said Ashley cautiously.

"Ar, reckon it will," Digby replied with a wide smile. Then he turned and plodded away. "Breakfast!" he muttered over his shoulder.

Ashley was alone on the bridge, feeling the warmth of the sun on his back. Slowly he picked up the empty box.

"Nice one, Uncle Leo!" he said as he looked at it. "You kept us waiting, but it was worth it!" Then he looked around him at the sun-splashed garden. "And, er, thanks, God," he added. "Thanks for your light ... I'm on your side now." His stomach growled loudly and he turned towards the house.

Chapter 14

Breakfast that morning turned into a celebration. When Mrs Latchett arrived, she came in to see what all the noise was about and stayed, wiping her eyes with her apron and murmuring, "Well I never! Who'd have thought it!" Tessa was trying to pour tea, but her eyes kept straying back to the heap of jewellery in the middle of the table. Meanwhile, Rachel was telling the whole story of the search, arms waving and cheeks flushed with excitement.

"Ashley knew we'd manage it," she gasped. "When I wanted to give up, he wouldn't let me."

"It wasn't me, really," Ashley wanted to be honest. "We *both* knew we had to keep trying."

"We had no idea you'd been so busy!" said Tessa, beaming at them both. "Mind you, I'm glad we didn't. I'd have been worried sick! What will your parents think of us, Ashley?"

"I don't think we did anything *really* dangerous," said Ashley modestly.

"Don't listen to him, Mum. He was *so* brave!" Rachel protested.

"Do you want to hear Uncle Leo's letter?" Patrick interrupted quietly. "I found this in the bottom of the box," he continued, waving a small, folded piece of paper. "Thank you, Ashley, for bringing it in, by the way." He smiled towards Ashley.

The room fell silent as Patrick cleared his throat and peered at the faded writing. "Dear Finder," he read...

"Have you enjoyed my little game? Perhaps you grew impatient with my methods, in which case I ask you to excuse an old man's eccentricities. It seems that the house has been in grave danger, for why else would you have started on this venture and persevered till now? Well done! I've no doubt you will know what to do with these beautiful things now that you have found them. They have been in our family for quite some time, and have adorned many a female Butterworth, now long gone. They are very precious, but I'm certain that the house they will save, and the good things that are done there, will have infinitely more value, both in this life and the next.

God bless you,

Leo Butterworth."

"Oh, *Pat!*" Tessa sniffed loudly and squeezed her husband's hand.

Patrick smiled round at everyone, his glasses starting to mist up. "Time for a prayer, I think."

Everyone bowed their heads.

Ashley listened intently as Patrick spoke to God as though he were sitting in the room with them. Ashley wanted to be part of the prayer, so he said a very firm "Amen!" with everyone else at the end.

So, God was on our side? He's interested in what's been going on here, and he didn't want Yaffle House to close? Seems like he didn't want Pig Face to win either.

"And now I need to make a few phone calls," said Patrick as he quietly left the room.

"Just fancy," said Mrs Latchett. "Those beautiful things were out there in the woods all those years and nobody knew." She shook her head in disbelief.

"Uncle Leo knew," Tessa pointed out, "but he was extremely good at keeping secrets."

"He wasn't the only one!" said Rachel, looking across at Ashley.

"Digby, you mean?" he said.

She nodded.

"If he knew, why didn't he tell us straight away?" said Ashley.

"I think he sort of ... forgot," Rachel replied.

"Oh yeah?"

"No, really. Remember, he was very young when Uncle Leo hid his loot. Maybe he didn't understand or remember till..."

"Till it was the right time?"

Rachel nodded. "I think that it was important to do all that hard work. If it'd all been really easy, we wouldn't be so happy now."

"We nearly gave up, though," Ashley continued.

"But something kept us going," Rachel reminded him firmly.

"It's what you call 'faith'," Tessa said, smiling. "Believing even when you don't understand and things seem hopeless."

"We can do the work on the house now though, can't we?" asked Rachel.

Tessa nodded. "We'll need to have the jewellery valued and find someone to sell it for us – but, yes, there'll be more than enough money to do all the repairs." She stretched her arms. "It's *such* a relief!

Oh goodness, it's time for the guests' breakfasts!"
She and Mrs Latchett hurried to the kitchen.

Slowly Rachel and Ashley wandered back outside.

"I'm *so* tired!" sighed Rachel as they crossed the courtyard.

"So am I," Ashley said. He threw a stick for the Mole. "It's like we've been carrying something very heavy for days."

As they turned the corner of the house, they looked down towards the lane. Sunlight glinted off a dark-blue car parked on the other side of the hedge.

"It's him!" said Rachel, sharply.

Ashley laughed. "You don't need to worry about Pig Face any more!"

Rachel relaxed. "I forgot. Whenever I see him, my tummy goes all tight."

They strolled down and peered through the hedge. Mr Doubleby was sitting in his car with the windows down. They could hear him talking on his phone.

"Just popped down to Beech Lane. Yah ... yah ... It's time to make a move, I think. We've given them long enough. What? ... Oh don't worry – the house is as good as ours!"

Ashley and Rachel looked at each other and grinned.

"I'd love to see his face when he hears!" said Rachel.

"Butterworths one, Pig Face nil!" Ashley chuckled.

The blue car moved off, a big shiny beetle scurrying back under a stone.

Ashley sat on the edge of his bed. He was packing,

ready to go home in the evening. The last few days had flown by as the jewellery was valued and phone calls were made to builders and decorators. The atmosphere had bubbled with happiness. Not only was Yaffle House safe, but there had been enough money to repair the Village Hall roof. There would be no leaks next winter and the play-group would still have a home. Uncle Leo's treasure had helped the whole village. Ashley picked up a pile of clothes and lifted the lid of his suitcase. There lay his Game Boy and a pile of comics, forgotten.

And I thought the country would be boring! It messes up your clothes and you have to go miles to find a shop, but it's the most exciting place I've ever been!

Rachel came in. She looked at his suitcase and pulled a face. "Wish you didn't have to go."

"Me too," he agreed.

"You're going to come again at half-term, aren't you?"

Ashley nodded, then he changed the subject. He had something on his mind.

"I'm a bit worried about going home," he confessed. "Not about seeing Mum and Dad; but starting school again," he explained. "I'm not sure I'll be able to keep the dark away."

"Jesus will help you," Rachel reminded him.

"I s'pose so," said Ashley doubtfully, "but I'll be all on my own. It's easy here, because there's you and Patrick and Tessa."

"Dad knows someone who goes to a church near where you live," said Rachel. "They have a club for people our age. I went to it last time we visited

Granny and Grandad. It's really good. You could go there. I'll ask Dad."

Ashley nodded.

"And don't forget," Rachel added, "Jesus is with you all the time, everywhere. He promised!"

"All the time, everywhere. He promised," Ashley repeated as he reached down and pulled his Walkman out from under the bed.

However slowly you do things, eventually the moment comes when you have to leave. "We really must go now," Patrick slammed the car boot shut. He was driving Ashley part of the way home, and Mum had arranged to meet them at a service area near one of the junctions on the motorway. A small dot by a curving blue line on a map. It didn't seem real. Rachel was coming to keep Patrick company on the journey back.

Ashley had gone to say goodbye to Digby earlier that afternoon

"Goin' back, then?"

Ashley nodded and made a face.

"Reckon you're a countryman at 'eart."

"P'raps."

"You'll be back."

"Hope so."

Digby laughed a silent laugh and turned back to his hoeing.

"Bye! Safe journey!" Tessa waved, holding the Mole firmly under her arm as the car scrunched over the gravel to the gate. Ashley looked back and saw the old house standing in the afternoon sunlight. He was glad that it was safe again and that he had been able to help.

The sun shone as they travelled the narrow lanes that gradually became roads and eventually led to the motorway. Ashley was sunk in his seat, hardly speaking as Rachel chattered brightly.

"This weather is a bit different from the day you arrived," said Patrick.

"Mm," replied Ashley.

"Enjoyed yourself?"

"Yes, it's been great."

"We'll never forget your visit," Patrick continued.

"Yes! Thanks to Sherlock, we found Uncle Leo's loot!" Rachel chipped in from the back seat.

Ashley shrugged. "It's like Uncle Leo said, the house is special. Good things happen in it. I wanted to make sure they kept happening."

Ashley's mum hadn't arrived when they reached the service area.

"Roadworks further north," said Patrick, listening intently to the car radio. "That'll have delayed her. We'll go and get a drink while we wait."

The sun was slowly setting as they walked through the car park towards the restaurant. Patrick bought two milkshakes and a coffee, and they took them to a table by the window.

"I'm going to use the phone," he said.

Rachel drank her milkshake while Ashley fiddled with his straw, thinking.

"Finding the loot was exciting, wasn't it?" said Rachel, slurping loudly.

"No one's going to believe me when I tell them!" Ashley laughed.

"Think of me, puffing along on my bike to Askew's store next time you go to the shopping mall!"

Ashley smiled. It wouldn't be *so* bad to go home. "I hope I can handle Jax."

"You'll be OK," Rachel reassured him as she licked the froth from her straw. "Don't forget – Dad's friend said he'll come and see you and tell you about the club."

"I'm coming back at half-term, too," Ashley added.

"And remember, you're taking Jesus and the light with you."

"Yes, I've got him with me all the time, every-where..."

"He *promised!*" they said together. Rachel flicked her straw at him and he ducked. Then looking through the window, he saw a familiar car edging its way into a parking space.

"Here's Mum!" he said, jumping up and waving.